"BLAKELY'S WRITING
UNDERSCORED WITH
MEN

"The   er
in the   s,
and t   y
genui

"Plen   y,
and a   i-
cal n   ce

"He   ve
and f   he
swift

"Bla   he
Western. Readers will hear more from him, and all of it will be
good."   —Norman Zollinger, author of *Not of War Only*

"An exciting, suspenseful novel with well-fleshed characters
and several surprises.... The gunfights and breaking-in of
mustangs are breathtaking."
                    —*Library Journal* on *The Snowy Range Gang*

By Mike Blakely
from Tom Doherty Associates

Comanche Dawn
Come Sundown
Dead Reckoning
Forever Texas
The Last Chance
Moon Medicine
Shortgrass Song
The Snowy Range Gang
Spanish Blood
Summer of Pearls
Too Long at the Dance
Vendetta Gold

DEAD RECKONING

Mike Blakely

TOR

A TOM DOHERTY ASSOCIATES BOOK
NEW YORK

This is a work of fiction. All the characters and events portrayed in this book are either products of the author's imagination or are used fictitiously.

DEAD RECKONING

Copyright © 1996 by Mike Blakely

Cover art by Jeffrey Terreson

A Forge Book
Published by Tom Doherty Associates, LLC
175 Fifth Avenue
New York, NY 10010

www.tor-forge.com

Forge® is a registered trademark of Tom Doherty Associates, LLC.

ISBN 978-0-8125-4830-3

First Edition: January 1977

Printed in the United States of America

0 9 8 7 6 5 4 3

One

❧

Dee Hassard shifted his rear end across the wagon bed, trying to avoid the splinters that angled from the rough boards. The cuffs behind his back held him to the steel springs of the buckboard seat, and the back of the seat bounced down on his shoulders every time the wheels hit a rough spot in the road. He sat backward in the wagon box, looking over the tailgate at the road winding snakelike through South Park.

"People are just so damned gullible," he said.

Frank Moncrief glanced over his right shoulder at his prisoner. "Plain stupid to fall for what you tried to pull," he replied. He looked beyond the two-mule team, scanning a timbered ridge a half mile ahead. This prisoner didn't have any partners coming to rescue him as far as Moncrief knew, but it didn't hurt to be watchful.

Hassard's leg irons rattled across the wagon bed as he squirmed for comfort. "You'd be surprised," he said.

"It's the smart ones that're most gullible. They're easier to get intrigued. They're ambitious. They're not necessarily greedy, but they'll risk a small fortune if they think there's profit in it."

Moncrief's eyes swept the horizon for smoke, dust, buzzards—anything that might warn or inform him. He saw only the snow-capped peaks of the distant ranges, the hacklelike timber on the high rolls, the great verdant grasslands guiding the South Platte through its undulations.

Crisp air cooled his nostrils, his throat, his lungs, charging him with something close to rapture. This place was big and simple, the way Frank Moncrief liked to live. It was primary, right down to the broad swaths of color—the bracing blue sky, the succulent green slopes, the icy whites of clouds and mountaintops—flecks of it all reflected in the blackness of the lucid river.

It galled him to be here on this wagon. He would much prefer a saddle. After he delivered Dee Hassard to the state penitentiary in Cañon City, he was going to trade his old buckboard and mule team for a good horse. He would take his time riding back to Fairplay, straying off this beaten trace to look over the hills when the notion struck him. He could almost feel the rhythm of the lope now.

"You can soak any ol' half-wit for a couple of greenbacks," Hassard continued, "but if you want to run a high-dollar confidence game, you have to go after somebody rich. And how do you think they got rich away out here in Colorado Territory? Well, not by bein' stupid. But not by playin' it safe, either."

"Still," Moncrief said. "Diamonds in South Park? I don't see how you pulled it off as long as you did."

"Hard work," Hassard said. "I know you think that's a line of bull—a confidence man workin' hard at anything—but it's true. You can't make it look too simple or too easy, or the mark will catch on. You've got to make it look complicated, like any other kind of business.

"Now, with the South Park Diamond Field, what I did was, I let my victims come to me. After I brought that first diamond into town and let the word slip out, I made myself scarce. I'd sneak out of town at night and give the slip to anybody tried to follow me. Mystery, Sheriff Moncrief, that's what got 'em. When the report came back from that jeweler in Denver that I had sure 'nough found a raw diamond, then all I had to do was wait."

Moncrief glanced down at the cuffs around the seat springs. He wasn't taking any chances with this flimflam artist. Hassard was built scrawny, but he had a tricky look about him. He stood only about five-seven, weighed maybe a hundred fifty with the cuffs and leg irons. But little men often knew how to equalize.

Moncrief had been on the trail of some road agents and hadn't taken part in Hassard's arrest or trial, but his deputy had briefed him. Hassard had been cooperative. He hadn't put up a fight during the arrest. Hadn't tried to escape. Pleaded guilty. But he was too damn sure of himself. Too casual. The man was going to prison with higher spirits than most men took into whorehouses.

"Was that diamond real," Moncrief asked, "or was the report from Denver faked?"

"The diamond was real."

"Where'd you get a real diamond, uncut like that?"

Hassard chuckled. "This ain't my first game, Sheriff. I got it and a dozen more like it off a jeweler back east on another job. Fenced the rest of 'em and kept the one for this swindle."

Moncrief hissed. " 'Swindle,' my foot. Plain ol' stealin' is what it was."

"Now, I resent that, Sheriff. A regular thief would have just broke into Sam Cornelius's saloon and robbed the till. My way of takin' his money was slicker, more daring. And I got more money than any sneak thief ever could have. But you gotta work hard at it. When Cornelius offered to buy the diamond field from me, I could have took him up on it right away and lit out with the

money. But I strung him along. I wouldn't have nothin'
to do with him at first. Didn't want to look too anxious.
After his price got high enough, I agreed."

Moncrief snorted his amusement. Sam Cornelius was
one hell of a saloon operator, but what did he know about
diamonds? "You mean he handed over all that gold dust?
Just like that?"

"Hell, no. He was too smart for that. He wanted to see
the diamond field first. So I blindfolded him and took him
to it. I had salted it with a bunch of worthless pieces of
agate, but he didn't know one rock from another. When
we got back to town, I showed him all sorts of forged
documents and contracts from the gemstone companies
in New York. That hooked him. He paid me the gold dust
then, and I got the hell out of Fairplay."

Moncrief could not hold back the chuckle. "Diamonds
in South Park!"

"Why not? They got diamonds in Arkansas, don't
they? I'm tellin' you, it was the slickest piece of work I
ever did."

"Then how come you got caught?"

Hassard spat over the side of the wagon. "Because that
tricky bastard Cornelius stole one of my fake diamonds
from the diamond field. I found out later that he had a
hole in the sole of his boot, and he stepped on top of one
of those agates I had showed him and pushed it up in the
toe of his boot. He knew that if he'd have tried just
pickin' it up, I'd have seen him. Anyway, he tried to sell
it in Denver, and a jeweler told him it wasn't worth a
damn. They tracked me down before I could board the
train to San Francisco. If Sam Cornelius hadn't been a
thief, I'd have gotten away with it all. But there went
three months of hard work in Fairplay wasted."

Frank Moncrief grunted. "Well, you won't have to do
any more of that hard work for a spell," he said, turning
to locate a hawk he had heard scream in the sky. "You
can take it easy, bustin' rocks in Cañon City for the next
five years."

The wheels of the buckboard hit a washed-out place in the road, slamming the spring seat down on Hassard's shoulder. "Ain't that a hell of a deal?" he said, grimacing through the pain. "It ain't like I murdered somebody. Hell, I never hurt nobody in my life. I met fellas in Fairplay who have shot and killed men over cards, and they're still walkin' free. And me, I pull a little swindle and get five years, hard labor."

Frank Moncrief drove the wagon around an easy bend in the road and saw the campground come into view. There the road veered away from the river, over the dry prairie toward Cañon City. It was early in the afternoon yet, but the mules had been pulling since dawn and needed rest. Anyway, this was the recognized campground on the Fairplay to Cañon City road, and Frank Moncrief liked it. Sleeping by the river would beat making a dry camp out in the open park. The stars would come out tonight like gems in Dee Hassard's fake field of diamonds.

"Maybe if you'd have given the money back, you might have gotten off a little lighter," Moncrief said.

"I tried to explain to 'em that I lost the money to a gambler in Denver. He cheated me blind, Sheriff Moncrief. I swear, there are so many crooks in this territory a man can't earn a living. When I get out of prison, I'm goin' back east."

"You'll stay out of those confidence games if you know what's good for you," Moncrief warned.

Hassard shook his head. "I'm too set in my ways."

"You're a young man yet."

"Yeah, but I've been workin' angles since I was a kid. People don't change, Sheriff. You ought to know that in your line of work."

Moncrief drove the wagon down next to the river and pulled the reins back. The bank wasn't steep here in the level park; the river looked like a manicured irrigation canal except for its aimless meanderings. "My brother sure did," he said, setting the brake. "I once drove him on this same route, cuffed to the wagon, just the way you are. And this is where we camped together the day before I put him in prison."

Hassard craned his neck and looked Moncrief in the eye for the first time that day. "Your own brother?"

"That's right." He grabbed his bedroll from the wagon box and threw it down on a patch of soft grass. "He was a hired gun for the Bayou Salado Ranch years ago. Wild as a drunken buck back then. Killed a few rustlers here and there."

Out of habit, the law man began walking a broad circle around the campground, looking for tracks coming or going. Had someone been here today? Yesterday? Could somebody have concealed a gun for Hassard to use on him in the night? Hassard didn't have a partner in the territory that he knew of, but confidence men often worked in pairs or in teams. He wasn't taking any chances. Satisfied that the camp had not been used in a week, Moncrief returned to the wagon, took the hobbles from the bed, and went to fix them on the mules.

"Killed a few rustlers, huh?" the prisoner said. "So, you jailed your own brother for murder."

"Naw, nobody cared about a few dead rustlers," the lawman answered. "But he stayed drunk too often, got fired, and went to rustlin' the ranch's cattle himself. I figured I better arrest him and get him tried before he wound up lynched."

"Your own brother . . ." Hassard lay on his side behind the buckboard seat. It felt good to stop here, get the weight off his hind end for a change.

"Best thing ever happened to him. He got religion down there in prison. Made a preacher. Maybe you've heard of him. Name's Carrol."

Hassard's chains rattled as he squirmed to a sitting position. "Carrol Moncrief, the fightin' parson? He's your brother?"

"Full blood."

"Well, I'll be damned. Wasn't he in on some big fight this spring?"

"He shot a couple of hard cases who tried to steal some horses from a camp meetin' he was preachin' outside of Pueblo. Just winged 'em."

Hassard chuckled. "Don't sound like he's settled down much to me."

"Oh, he's changed. Before he got religion, he'd just as soon kill you as look at you, and he'd do about anything for a dollar. He was a sight worse than you, Hassard. You said yourself you never hurt nobody in your life. Carrol's done worse than hurt folks. That's why I say you can mend your ways. If Carrol Moncrief did, you can, too."

Hassard shrugged and lay back down on his side. "What's he doin' with hisself these days?"

Moncrief slipped the bit from a mule's mouth and let the beast wander off to graze. "He rides a circuit all through the territory. Preaches at weddings and funerals and camp meetings. Picks up a dollar here, dollar there. Got a letter from him last week. Said he hired on to guide some bunch of religious fanatics from Clear Creek over to the Western slopes."

"Religious fanatics?"

"Yeah, the Church of the Weeping Virgin, or some such name as that. From the states. They want to build their own town out in the wilderness. Be lucky if the Indians don't slaughter 'em all. Anyway, Carrol is supposed to meet 'em on Clear Creek and guide 'em over the mountains."

Hassard lay on his side in silence. He could just see the fighting parson taking a band of fanatics over the divide. Odd things happened out here. That's why this was such fertile ground. People here would fall for things like diamonds lying around on the ground in South Park. "Hey, Sheriff," he said suddenly. "You gonna let me loose so I can accomplish my toilet?"

The lawman dropped the wagon tongue and reached

into his coat pocket for the keys. "Never heard it said that way."

"You have to learn to talk like that if you want to bamboozle those rich Easterners. You'd never know it to look at me now, but I can clean up like the starchiest dandy you ever seen," Hassard claimed.

Moncrief unlocked the cuffs. "Get out," he ordered. He looked the swindler over as he watched him rub his wrists and climb out of the wagon bed. The reddish-blond stubble on the man's face, the tattered wool suit, and the moth-eaten hat made it difficult indeed to see him as an Eastern dude. "Hold your hands out," he said.

Hassard put his wrists together in front of him and let Moncrief fasten the cuffs again. "I'll only be a couple of minutes, then I'll help you set up camp."

"I'll do it myself. You'll stay cuffed to the wagon."

Hassard shrugged and turned toward the river. He ambled toward a patch of cattails downstream and downwind, the chain straightening between his ankles with every stride. He followed a narrow path into the cattails, the obvious latrine location for the campsite. He knew it well. He had memorized every step of this trail before he ever set foot in Fairplay. The South Park Diamond Field scam really was the slickest piece of work Dee Hassard had ever pulled off, and it wasn't over yet.

He found the rock he had planted there before and stopped beside it. He looked back toward the wagon, saw Moncrief watching him over the back of the second mule. He unbuttoned his pants, letting them drop to his ankles. He squatted, and Deputy Frank Moncrief disappeared behind the veil of cattails.

The stone between his feet rolled over easily, revealing the bundle of oilcloth pressed into the soft ground. He picked it up, trying to keep the cuffs from rattling as he pulled back the folds, revealing the .36-caliber Smith & Wesson revolver. A few specks of rust had appeared on the blue gunmetal, but otherwise the pistol seemed no worse for the wait.

When Hassard came out of the cattails, Frank Moncrief was throwing firewood out of the wagon bed. The lawman had stopped to gather the wood in the timber on one of the high rolls. "You want to sit on the seat, or on the ground?" the sheriff asked.

"The ground, I guess," Hassard said, approaching. He saw the deputy reach into his pocket for the keys. "You'll never guess what I found over there," he said.

"A diamond?" Moncrief answered.

"Somethin' more valuable than that." Hassard reached into his coat and put his hand on the revolver stuck in his waistband. He saw the key drop from Moncrief's hand. He pulled the weapon out, grasping it in both hands.

Moncrief froze with his hand on his sidearm. He heard the wind moaning among the wheel spokes. That hawk screamed down on him again. "You're makin' a mistake, Hassard," he said.

The confidence man showed his straight white teeth and chuckled. "Take off your gun belt and throw it over here."

"No." He saw his mistake now. He had stopped to camp at a recognized campground. He should have chosen some random site.

"I'll kill you if you don't."

"You're liable to try killin' me if I do, but you better think hard about it. That gun's been out there in the cattails a while from the looks of it. It might misfire."

"It might. You a gamblin' man?"

"If it shoots, you think one shot from a thirty-six cal will kill me?"

Hassard's eyes twinkled. "It's been known to happen."

"All right, say it does happen. Say you kill me. You'll just make things worse. You're not a murderer, Hassard, you're just a two-bit confidence artist."

Hassard sighed. "I think I better clear somethin' up with you, Moncrief. You remember before, when I said I had never hurt nobody in my life?"

"I remember."

"I lied." He tightened his finger on the trigger.

The mules leaped when the pistol fired, one of them almost throwing itself down, its front legs hobbled together as they were. Moncrief fell back against the wagon and slumped to the ground, blood gushing from his head wound.

Hassard cocked the pistol and watched. The lawman kept breathing for a couple of minutes, but Hassard just waited. Another shot might alert somebody, he thought. Probably not, but it didn't hurt to be careful. When he was sure Moncrief was dead, he put the pistol in the wagon bed and reached into the lawman's pocket for the keys.

The gun belt was hard to drag out from under the dead weight of the body, and when he strapped it on, he found that it needed a new hole for the buckle, his waist being much thinner than Moncrief's. He fished a pocket-knife from Moncrief's pants and sat down to bore the new hole.

He looked at the dead body and shook his head. "It's a wonder what some people won't fall for," he said.

Two

✦

Sister Petra knelt at the altar of the tiny adobe chapel, her fingers moving methodically from one rosary bead to the next. She whispered the prayers unconsciously, her eyelids quivering. Her neck ached from bowing to the crucifix on the rude wall. Her knees throbbed with pain, even on the goose-down pillow she had brought from her room. But she felt little of this world, heard her own whispers only as an echo of something far distant.

Suddenly she fell still and silent, no one watching her, no world existing for her beyond the adobe walls. "Amen," she said, her voice snapping the trance. She had prayed alone, from dawn to dusk, for nine straight days. Now it was in the hands of God.

The sun had fallen behind the Sangre de Cristos, and light had grown dim in the chapel. Sister Petra opened her eyes and stared at the gray shadows. After nine days, her mind had become as a clock, able to sense sundown as if she had watched it happen.

She pushed herself up from the altar, rubbing her sore knees. Hunger growled in her stomach, and she smiled. She hadn't felt this carefree in weeks. Now the answer would come. If the village of Guajolote died and blew away with the dust, it was God's will.

The Ojo de los Brazos land grant had been acquired by American land speculators in Santa Fe. Guajolote and almost forty-five hundred acres surrounding it were for sale. The sage plains where the villagers grazed their herds and flocks: for sale. The mountain slopes where they hunted and gathered wood: for sale. The beautiful springs in the foothills, pouring twin arms into the Mora River: all for sale. Even the earthen homes of the villagers were for sale, and Sister Petra had learned that a prospective buyer was on his way from the states to view the grant.

"How can they do that?" José Villareal had demanded of her. "You are an Anglo. You know what they are doing." He was the village alcalde, and the news had quite understandably enraged him.

"But I don't know," Sister Petra had answered. "I don't understand it any more than you do."

"What are we going to do?"

"I will go to Santa Fe and find out."

So she had gone. She had found the speculator, an immaculate little American lawyer called Lefty Harless whose office stood near the Palace of the Governors.

"It's very simple, Sister," Harless had said matter-of-factly. "The county taxes were delinquent on the Ojo de los Brazos grant. I paid the taxes, thereby acquiring the land."

"But we've been paying the taxes regularly," Petra argued. "There must have been a mistake in the records."

"No mistake. The taxes went up in your county. You didn't pay at the new level."

"No one told us," she complained.

The lawyer shrugged. "It was published in the newspapers."

Petra gasped in frustration. "Mr. Harless, we are a remote village. Few of our people even read. We hardly ever see a newspaper."

"That's very unfortunate."

"How did you, in Santa Fe, manage to find out that our taxes were delinquent before we did in our own county?"

Harless picked at something between his teeth with his thumbnail. "I have friends in the county government up there."

Petra fumed. "I can see that you do." She pursed her lips and glared at the little cheat. "We'll pay you back. What did the tax increase amount to?"

Harless spread a smug smile across his face. "The taxes have gone back down to their original level, but that's hardly the point, Sister. I own the land now, and I intend to sell it to the first buyer who will pay my price."

"But what about the people?" Sister Petra snapped. "Do you think you've bought their souls? Have you sold your own?"

The speculator shifted his bloodshot eyes. "What do you mean by that?"

"What about the homes of the people, their village, their lives?"

Harless answered coolly. "It's a free market. Buy the grant yourself if you're so concerned about the village."

"How much?" she asked.

"A dollar twenty-five an acre."

Sister Petra had squinted her bright green eyes at the speculator. "But that's over five thousand dollars!"

"Fifty-six even," he had said.

That number had burdened her like a cross on the long walk around the mountains back to Guajolote. Fifty-six even! He had said it so casually, as if it were nothing! But by the time she returned to Guajolote, she knew what she would do. It was all very simple. Give it over to God. She would devote nine days of prayer to the matter—a novena.

And now the final day of her novena had passed, and she was free of the responsibility she had taken on for the village and its people. She picked up her pillow, walked to the door, looked down on the adobes perched along the bank of the generous Mora.

A rooster strutted in front of her. She lunged at it suddenly, hissing and waving her pillow. She laughed as the bird went cackling down the street.

The dry summer evening caressed her as she walked through the village, arching the stiffness from her back. It was a blessing to live here; one she too seldom gave thanks for. She would have to remember to thank God first thing tomorrow, but right now she was all prayed out. Kentucky would be in a muggy nighttime swelter, she mused. Dusk in New Mexico was Sister Petra's heaven.

She missed Kentucky sometimes: the greenery, the long cadence of rainfall on the shake roof, the lush aromas of moldering timber. But never did she regret leaving. Her purpose was here.

She had lived in Guajolote five years now, and was loved by everyone—even that old politician José Villareal, who resented the people seeking the advice of Sister Petra above his.

She had done everything she knew to save the village from the speculators. If the grant sold, and the villagers lost their homes, it would be the will of God.

She had started her first day of prayer asking only that the will of God be done. But now she realized, as she followed the frightened rooster down into the village, that she had asked for something very different on this ninth day of prayer. It was just a vague recollection now, in this world of earthly toil, but she had been praying all day for a number.

She didn't care to speak to anyone as she made her way through the village. She was too exhausted to even seek a greeting. She wanted only a meal and a long night's sleep.

"Is it nine days now, Sister?" the voice said.

She saw José Villareal sitting against the wall of his house. "Yes," she said. "God is making up his mind what to do with your village now. I hope you will be ready."

The alcalde chuckled. "Bless you, Sister Petra. I don't think all your praying will do any good, but I will remember that you tried."

"Only good comes of prayer. It may not seem good to us, but we cannot see as much as God."

"Go get some rest," the alcalde said, waving her away. "You are not making any sense."

She was starving when she reached her door. How long had it been since she ate well? How much sleep had she gotten over the past nine days? It had been fitful sleep, reciting Hail Marys and Our Fathers in her dreams. What was that number she had prayed for all day? Her mind was numb. She couldn't remember.

When she opened her door, she smelled the aromas of tortillas and *queso* in the tiny room, and it made her smile. Some kind woman had made something for her. She lit the candle, found a flask of wine beside a basket of food.

She filled a cup. The wine would strengthen her, give her energy to stay awake long enough to eat. The first sip was like a balm, and she recalled, suddenly, the number: "fifty-six even." Just as the land speculator in Santa Fe had said it. Had she been wise to pray so for money?

"You should be careful what you pray for," she said to herself in English. That was strange. She hadn't spoken a word of English aloud since Santa Fe.

The wineglass slipped from Petra's hand, and she faintly heard it shattering. A blinding white light had burst into the room, consuming her. And as she floated, she felt the warm voice of God surging through her flesh, rattling her very bones:

"The cross awaits you on the mountainside."

Three

❧

He stood on a high roll of the grassy plains, his arms folded across his chest, cradling his Remington rolling-block hunting rifle. The sky was pink in the west, purple above him, charcoal gray in the east. He simply stared at it with his mouth open, his eyes sweeping ceaselessly across it.

Clarence Philbrick had been brought up in Vermont, where the sky was a patch of benevolent ether hemmed in overhead by treetops. But here the great void had beaten back everything and swelled to the point that Clarence felt as if he were standing naked on a liberty dime.

He stared silently, mentally composing an entry for his diary as he tried to soak in the infinity of it all. Back east, he mused, my view of the sky was like that of a trout searching the surface of his dark pool for mayflies. But here I am as a wild soaring goose, enveloped in tideless reaches of oxygen.

Clarence couldn't help thinking of things in terms of fish and game.

A ladle clanged against an iron pot down the slope, and he turned toward camp. He had built up a powerful hunger skinning buffalo all day, and now he was ready for some hump stew and that delicacy of the plains—boiled tongue. He saw the line of hunters forming at the cook's cauldron and hoped they would leave some cornbread for him.

It was getting cooler now with the night coming on, and Clarence was glad. It was hard to wear his oilskin hunting coat when the sun got high, and if he didn't wear it, he had to keep it rolled under his arm when he walked, tied behind his saddle when he rode, or pinned under his knee while he skinned buffalo. The idea was to prevent anyone from picking up his coat for whatever reason and feeling its heft. Clarence had twenty-one pounds of gold sewn into his coat, and he would just as soon nobody knew about it.

He had gotten the idea from his father, Herbert Philbrick, who had gone to California back in '49 and struck a rich placer load near Mariposa. Herbert had melted his gold dust into bars and sewn them into his coat before returning to Vermont. He had hired on as a deckhand for the homeward voyage, so no one would suspect the wealth he carried.

Clarence's father had put quite a sum of money away for him in a trust fund, which he wasn't to touch until he was thirty-five years old. "Nobody has any sense until they're thirty-five years old," Herbert had said. "And damned little then."

But more so than the gold, Clarence treasured the stories his father had brought back from California. He made his father repeat often how he had fought off claim-jumpers and thieves; made a fortune with a pick, a pan, and sweat; survived two trips around the Horn. The stories made Clarence anxious to go west himself, to have his own adventures, but the adventures he had in mind would require capital.

"Go on if you want to," his father had said. "I'm not stopping you. It'll be good for you. Make a man of you."

Clarence was twenty-five and considered himself a man already. "But I need the money," he tried to explain.

The old forty-niner smiled and puffed on his pipe. "I left for California with three dollars and fifty-seven cents in my pocket. I'll stake you to the same amount."

Clarence had thrown his arms in the air and flung himself against the bookshelf in his father's study. "But you've said yourself there will never be another gold strike like California. It's cattle now, and a man needs capital to buy his first spread. The panic has driven land prices lower than they've been in years. Now is the time to invest."

He had left it there, exasperated, and stormed out of his father's study. Weeks later, his father called him back in to show him something.

"Look what Senator White gave me today, son. It's a photograph. Have you ever seen anything like it?"

Clarence had taken the large print and looked at it—like looking out through a window across the continent. Every grain was like a living atom, and the scene swept him back through all the lost moments since the shutter opened, casting him out through the very lens of the photographer's camera.

He found himself standing on high ground, the rocky grades around him devoid of life, windswept, streaked with snow. But it was the cross that made him shiver. Etched in new-fallen snow, it spanned one whole side of the highest peak in view, settling comfortably into natural time-carved crevices.

"What is this place?" Clarence had asked.

"It's a mountain peak out west. Colorado, I think. The chief photographer of the Hayden Survey made the picture. Senator White gave me his copy."

"You see, that's why I need the money!" Clarence

blurted. "I'm missing these sights! I'm missing everything!"

He had persisted, day after day, week after week, until finally his father had agreed to a compromise.

"All right, Clarence," the elder Philbrick said, "I'll let you have five thousand dollars to get you started in the cattle business. If you lose it, that's tough. I will not, on my life, let you have one cent more until you are thirty-five."

Herbert Philbrick fully expected his son to lose every penny of that five thousand. The boy had no business sense and no aptitude for anything besides fishing and hunting. But he thought of it as an investment in his son's education. Once the boy went broke, he would have to learn fast out there—or die.

Clarence was so thrilled the day his father offered the compromise that he ran down to Lake Champlain and went swimming, though it was April and the water was frigid. He began writing letters before he had even dried off, and within two months had found a ranch in his price range in the Territory of New Mexico. The brochure sent to him by a land speculator named Lefty Harless described the spread:

"The legendary Ojo de los Brazos League . . . granted by the government of Spain in 1814 . . . confirmed by act of Congress of the United States . . . nestled among the foothills of the Sangre de Cristos Mountains, flanking five miles of the Mora River . . . It encompasses 4,480 acres of prime grazing land, hundreds of which might be brought into a high degree of cultivation. . . . Surrounding the grant are hundreds of thousands of acres of free government range. . . . The Ojo de los Brazos League includes a Mexican village called Guajolote, which might be exploited for its peasant workforce or removed from the ranch."

The price was six hundred dollars over the five thousand Clarence's father had promised him, so he had to sell his collection of fowling guns and fly rods to raise

the remainder. The only gun he kept was his Remington
rolling-block hunting rifle. To pay for the trip west, he
had to sell his favorite Morgan stallion and all his riding
tack. He understood that the English saddle would be
frowned upon out west, anyway.

By the end of June, he still didn't have train and stagecoach fare to get him all the way to New Mexico, but
Clarence could wait no longer. He wanted to be in posses-
sion of the Ojo de los Brazos well before autumn. Lefty
Harless insisted on being paid in gold coin, fearing the
panic would lessen the value of paper money. As there
were no banks or railroads in New Mexico, Clarence had
to make his own arrangements for getting the gold to
Sante Fe.

"Do what I did," his father suggested. "Sew it into your
jacket."

So Clarence converted his fifty-six hundred to twenty-
dollar gold pieces—280 double eagles weighing almost
twenty-one pounds. These his mother quilted into the
lining of his favorite oilskin hunting jacket. She paired
the coins, sewing four rows down the front, two rows in
each sleeve, and six rows across the back.

"Dress like a common workman, and travel cheap," his
father advised. "Don't let that jacket get beyond your
grasp, and above all, do not let anybody pick it up."

The young Vermonter headed west on the rails in early
July. He stretched his spending money as far as it would
go, but arrived in Denver broke, save for the gold sewn
into his coat. He met some sportsmen heading out onto
the plains to hunt buffalo and hired on with them as a
skinner. He had field-dressed a lot of deer back east and
figured skinning a buffalo would be no more difficult.

It turned out to be a good deal more difficult owing to
the size of the animals and the humps on their backs, but
Clarence worked hard and learned fast. The third day of
the hunt, some of the sportsmen accidentally stampeded a
small herd of bison past their skinner, and Clarence killed
a big cow with his Remington.

So it was that Clarence Philbrick strolled down to the camp cook's kettle now feeling like a seasoned plainsman. His clothes were bloodstained, his hands tanned on the backs and blistered on the palms. He swaggered to the end of the grub line and left his Remington leaning against a wagon box.

"See anything up there?" asked one of the hunters, a man from Illinois.

Clarence shook his head. "Sky and grass."

The hunting guide stepped up beside Clarence holding a tin plate of stew. He wore his hair and mustaches long. "Better turn in early tonight. We leave for Denver before dawn."

"Yes, sir," Clarence answered.

"I'm goin' right back out with another party if you want to hire on again. You can double your wages."

Clarence fought back a prideful smile. "Thanks, but I need to be getting on to New Mexico. I've got a job waiting down there on a ranch."

The plainsman nodded. "I'll pay you when we get to town. You'll have about fifteen dollars comin'."

Clarence grinned and picked up a plate. "Been a long time since I had that much money in my pocket," he said. He held his plate out to the cook and glanced across the tailgate of the chuck wagon. "Any cornbread left?" he asked.

The cook sneered. "Some of them greedy bastards took two," he said under his breath.

Clarence shrugged, poured himself a cup of black coffee, and went to sit on the bed of the wagon where he had left his Remington. He ran the journal entry through his mind again so he wouldn't forget it: . . . a trout in his dark pool . . . searching for mayflies . . . a wild soaring goose . . . tideless reaches of oxygen.

When he got back to Denver in a couple of days, he would have a bath and buy a train ticket as far south as the tracks went. Pueblo, he had been told. But before he boarded the train, there was something he wanted to do.

It wasn't the sort of thing he would want to enter into his diary, but he was on his own out here. Who would know? Who would care? He was going to visit one of those fancy Denver whorehouses.

He remembered something the family gardener had once told him as they shared a bottle of port Clarence had smuggled out of the house: "It ain't how deep you fish, son, it's how you wiggle your worm." He smiled. Yes, Clarence thought, angling can be made to serve as a metaphor for almost anything.

Four

❧

The old mule was sore-footed from the long ride, but Dee Hassard awarded her no sympathy. He kept a switch busy across her rump and cussed her every time she slowed her walk. He had traded Frank Moncrief's other mule for an old saddle at Tarryall and had ridden down the South Platte toward Denver.

Now Denver was in sight below, and he was riding up to the rocky outcropping over Clear Creek where he had hidden the gold from the sale of the South Park Diamond Field. After he recovered Sam Cornelius's Fairplay dust, he would board an eastbound and live it up for a couple of months before his earnings played out.

He wondered if anybody had found Frank Moncrief's body yet. He had made a hearse of the sheriff's buckboard and left it over a hill, out of sight of the road. Even if somebody had found Moncrief by now, there was still

plenty of time to get away. The news could trave[l]
faster than a gallop.

He stood in the stirrups and stretched his neck, fo[r]
gold was close and he was looking for the place. It [was]
just over the ridge here somewhere, he recalled. A[s he]
approached the summit and spotted the rocky point,
eyes bulged. He shifted his reins to his left hand a[nd]
pulled back on them, putting his right palm on the gri[p of]
Frank Moncrief's Colt.

A man was seated on the outcropping, his foot [in]ches from the hole in which the Fairplay gold [was]
hidden. The man had his hands inside some sort of [box]
on a portable table. Nearby stood a fine white m[are]
wearing a saddle. Between them and the man stoo[d a]
tripod holding a black cube with a cloth hanging from [it.]

The man looked up, tossed his head, smiled. "How[dy,"]
he said, leaving his hands inside the box. His build [was]
compact, like Hassard's. He had sad eyes, wavy br[own]
hair, and a full beard, well trimmed.

"Howdy, yourself," Hassard said. He glanced d[own]
into the creek valley as he heard a faint line of son[g. A]
chorus was singing some hymn down there. He spo[tted]
the tents and wagons of a campground below, then gl[anced]
at the stranger with his hands in the box. "What you [got]
in there?"

"I'm washing a photographic plate," the man sai[d. "I]
just made a view of Clear Creek with Denver and [the]
prairies beyond."

Hassard nodded and took his hand off his gun g[rip.]
"What for?"

"It's my job," the man said, his beard revealin[g a]
smile. "I'm W. H. Jackson, head of the photogra[phic]
division of the Hayden Survey. I'd get up and shake y[our]
hand if I could."

"That's all right," Hassard said, getting down fro[m the]
mule. He rubbed his rear end. "I saw you down be[low]
and got curious. Thought you were some kind [of]
prospector or somethin'."

The confidence man looked down on the campground of the hymn singers again, lingering over it this time. He recognized the tune: "Will the Circle Be Unbroken." "Never saw a photograph bein' made before," he said.

"This is just the plate," Jackson explained. "I'll have to take it down to the studio to print photographs."

Hassard shot a quick glance at the hole under the rock where he had stashed his gold. "What the hell is the Hayden Survey?"

"Government geological explorations," the photographer said, "headed by Dr. Ferdinand Vandeveer Hayden."

"And you go around and make photographs of everything they explore?"

"Not everything. Just the points of interest." Jackson removed his hands from the box. "Maybe you've seen some of my photographs from Colter's Hell in the Yellowstone country."

Hassard put his hand on his chin. "You mean the geysers and hot springs and all?"

"Yes." He had opened the box and was removing a developed plate of glass.

Hassard stuck his thumbs under his gun belt and approached the photographer. "Now, tell me the truth, Jackson. Is that Yellowstone country for real? I can spot a hoax, you know, and them geysers don't set right with me."

"It's real, all right," Jackson said. "I brought the photographic evidence back to Congress. Why do you think they established the national park?" He put the exposed glass in a pan of fluid on a rock and wiped his fingers on his shirt.

"I figured it was some kind of government scam. What the hell do we need a national park for, anyhow?" He looked into the pan at the plate of glass, unable to see a picture in it. "I believe I've heard of this Hayden Survey before," he said. "Were you all in Fairplay last summer?"

"We were," Jackson said.

"I thought so. I was just there a few days ago. Folks are still talkin' about you-all down there. Said you was on some wild-goose chase to photograph some mountain cross, or holy snowy cross, or some such thing."

Jackson's sad eyes twinkled as he looked up from his work. "We found it," he said. "I was the first to photograph it."

"But what is it?" Hassard demanded.

Jackson stood erect, pointed west. "It was just a legend until we located it. I had talked to a lot of people who knew of it, but none who had ever seen it. Then, as luck would have it, we ran into an old prospector up in the Sawatch who claimed he had seen it once. He was lost when he stumbled across it, then he found his way, like magic."

"Stumbled across what?"

"The Mount of the Snowy Cross. The old man told us it was visible only from a few places above timberline. He said the best place to see it from was Notch Mountain, an easy landmark to recognize because of the notch in its summit. So I took the photographic division over the Great Divide at Tennessee Pass. There's an old Indian trail that leads from there past the base of Notch Mountain. We had to leave the mules below and carry the camera and chemicals and plates on our backs. A couple of miles above timberline, we finally came over the summit of Notch Mountain, and there it was, standing across a high mountain basin."

"There what was?" Hassard said.

"The snowy cross."

"But what the hell is it?"

Jackson put his feet together, stood straight, and spread his arms. "It's a huge cross formed by snow packed into natural crevices in the slope of a mountain peak. It stands a thousand feet tall." He let his palms rise above his shoulders. "The arms lift upward to heaven like this, hundreds of feet wide. The top of the cross reaches the very peak of the Mount of the Snowy Cross. I just got a glimpse of it before clouds moved in and obliterated it."

"I thought you said you got photographs of it."

"We had to camp on Notch Mountain overnight," Jackson said, letting his arms fall. "The next morning the clouds cleared long enough for me to make eight exposures. One of them was excellent. It was an extraordinary experience."

Silence surrounded the rocky outcropping over the creek, and Hassard found the image of the snowy cross on his mind now even clearer than that of the gold hidden at the photographer's feet. "I guess everybody knows about it now," he said. "Like them geysers up in Colter's Hell."

Jackson shrugged as he moved his glass plate to another pan of fluid. "The photograph circulated fairly well in certain circles back east, but oddly enough, the Snowy Cross is still thought of as a legend out here."

Hassard recognized a new tune in the valley below: "The Old Rugged Cross." "Funny they should start singin' that," he said.

"Not really," Jackson replied. "They do a lot of singing, and that's one of their favorites. We're camped not far down the creek from them, and I hear them singing several times a day."

"Who are they?"

"Some bunch of religious fanatics who call themselves the Church of the Weeping Virgin." Jackson took the glass plate from the pan of fluid and carried it to a box on the ground beside his pack mule. "Mind opening that lid for me?"

Hassard took the cover from the sturdy wooden box to reveal padded slots inside, most of them holding plates of glass. He held the lid as the photographer slid his negative into one of the empty slots. "The Church of the Weeping what?" The swindler's interest rose. Hadn't Frank Moncrief mentioned something about this?

Jackson motioned for Hassard to replace the lid on the

box and took a fresh plate of treated glass from a holder near the camera. "Weeping Virgin. They seem like simple Christian folks, but their late founder was an eccentric who claimed the angel of the Virgin Mary spoke to him in dreams."

Hassard chuckled. "What did the ol' girl say?"

The photographer was installing the plate of glass in his boxlike camera. "According to this prophet—his name was Wyckoff—she instructed all faithful Christians to renounce materialism and give all their money to the church, which seems awful convenient for Wyckoff, since he controlled the church finances. Also, he claimed the Virgin Mary said to shun outsiders but embrace anybody who accepted their religion. Well, that's what got them into trouble."

"How's that?"

"Wyckoff told his people they were going west to establish a new community in the wilderness. But before they did, they made a sweep across the southern states preaching and looking for converts. They let some black folks join."

"Alongside of white folks?" Hassard said.

Jackson nodded. "And worse. One of the white ladies from up north decided she wanted to marry one of the black men from down south. This Reverend Wyckoff said the Virgin Mary had told him that one day all the races would be as one, and so he married this couple in their camp somewhere in Arkansas. They were mobbed by some local thugs, the newlywed couple and Wyckoff lynched."

Hassard's eyebrows raised. "Who's leadin' 'em now?"

"They're waiting on a guide to take them into the mountains. A Reverend Carrol Moncrief. Maybe you've heard of him." Jackson put his head under the black cloth hanging from his camera.

"Sure," Hassard said, grinning. "He rides a circuit big as the territory. I met his brother down in Fairplay." He turned to look again at the hole under the rocky outcropping where his gold lay hidden. "You gonna make some more pictures?"

"Yes," Jackson said, coming out from under the hood. "The sun's good right now. Say, how would you like to get into one of them?"

"A photograph?" The swindler's smile broadened. It was something akin to becoming immortal, getting one's picture made. "It won't really steal my soul, will it?"

"Not unless your soul is very loose. Stand there on that boulder." The photographer glanced up to judge the light. "Quick, before that cloud covers the sun."

Hassard felt giddy as he stepped onto the boulder, the vast grasslands behind him. He held his coat back to reveal Frank Moncrief's gun belt and Colt revolver, his own rust-speckled Smith & Wesson tucked under the cartridge belt.

"Look at the camera," Jackson said.

Hassard raised one eyebrow. This was a little risky, he realized. He had heard of detectives using photographs to track people down. But Hassard made it a policy to change his appearance after every job, anyway. In that way, the photograph might actually help cover his trail. He heard the shutter open and close, felt the cloud shade him.

"What did you say your name was?" Jackson asked. "I try to identify my subjects when possible."

"Hassard. Dee Hassard." He heard the pilgrims strike up a new hymn in the valley below.

"And what is your profession?"

"Investments."

Jackson left it at that. "You're welcome to come down to the studio tomorrow and see a print."

"Thanks all the same," Hassard said, turning for his mule. "But I've got places to go. Good luck on your survey this summer."

"We're going down to the San Juans by way of Fairplay. Want me to pass anything along to anybody down there?"

Dee Hassard put his foot in the stirrup and climbed onto the weary mule. "I don't have any friends there," he said, smiling. "I was just passin' through." He touched his hat brim and reined his mount down the slope toward Denver.

He would have to come back later for the gold, but that didn't matter right now. The money didn't sway Dee Hassard the way the plotting did—all the risky conniving and the feeling of power he got when he made a slick escape, or even when he rescued a botched job like he had done in South Park.

And right now, he could feel an idea coming on. All those gullible Weeping Virgin idiots waiting for a new prophet down there in camp. He had never heard of the late Reverend Wyckoff, but he would have bet his entire diamond field haul that the good reverend was more confidence man than prophet.

Five

❧

May Tremaine's new shoes were not meant for walking. She had blisters on her feet the size of dimes—about two dollars' worth, judging by the sharp pains that stabbed her with every step.

Most of the stores and shops had shut down, late afternoon filling the streets of Denver with shadow. She felt tired and dirty. If she didn't find some work now, it would mean another night in the wagon yard, and that man there was going to expect reimbursement tonight. He had told her as much when she left this morning.

She saw a door ajar down the street and quickened her step, though it felt like walking barefoot over sharp rocks. The sign simply said HARDWARE, a commodity about which she knew nothing. She reached for the door, but it opened before she could grab the brass handle, and a man stepped onto the street.

"Sorry," he said. "Closed for the day."

"No, I'm looking for a job," May replied.

The man turned his key in the lock. "Well, we're not hiring." He turned to walk away.

"Wait!" May cried. "Please, wait."

The man stopped in the street and turned.

"I have no money. I have no place to stay. I'll work for room and board. Just until I find something else. Please. I'll do anything." She gestured toward the store, but she knew the man would take it the wrong way.

He smiled with one side of his mouth as his eyes traveled down her skirt and slowly back to her face. "My wife wouldn't approve of that sort of arrangement. Good luck." And he left, shaking his head as he walked away.

May thought about that man back in the wagon yard. It wouldn't be so bad. He had bathed last night, and had made sure she knew about it this morning, having worn oil in his hair and a clean shirt. But where would it get her? A restless night on a bed of straw? She would be better off hiring herself out as just a regular whore. At least then she would get paid.

Up until a couple of days ago, May thought she had made it in Denver. She had landed a job in a shoe shop, and the cobbler had advanced her a pair of shoes, as hers was pretty much worn out. The job had gone well for a week. Then, two days ago, while cleaning up after hours, the cobbler had followed her into the back room. When she reached up to put a pair of shoes on a high shelf, he grabbed her from behind, squeezing her breasts with both hands, pressing himself against her.

She had gasped and wrenched violently away, elbowing him in the mouth as she stumbled and fell to the ground. She sprang and ran, made it to the door, and bolted out to the street.

"Hey!" was all the cobbler said as she ran away.

She had made just enough money that week to earn the shoes that were giving her blisters now. She walked on. She wasn't going to sleep on that wagon yard straw again tonight.

May didn't know what she did to make men come after her like that. When she looked in the mirror, she didn't see a pretty woman. She thought her eyes and her lips were too large. Her face was too wide, her chin too weak. She had always wanted to be tall and skinny and able to run like a deer. But she was of medium height, too curvaceous to be considered skinny, even though she carried no extra weight. She didn't see herself as pretty, but men had been groping for her since she was fifteen.

It had started with her uncle, the husband of her mother's sister, an army captain back in Iowa. He was quite a dashing character, having done battle with Indians on the plains. It was true that May had flirted with him in a girlish way, but it never even remotely occurred to her that she might summon the monster in him. She was visiting on the army post for the summer, and her aunt had gone to town one day, leaving her alone in the captain's quarters. The captain came home in the middle of the morning, asked her to come into the bedroom, and pushed her onto the bed, falling on top of her.

"If you scream again, I'll hit you," he said, pressing his hand hard over her mouth. "You've been wanting this and now you're gonna get it." He felt like he weighed five hundred pounds on top of her. And though she cried the entire time, he seemed not to notice, and even told her how good she made him feel.

There were others who tried—men and boys—and she let the more persistent ones succeed. May came to believe that this was a terror all girls just suffered because men were bigger and stronger, and because they harbored that monster in their hearts. When she told her best friend about it, her friend never spoke to her again. Then she knew her life was different. It wasn't all girls; it was just she. She honestly did not know why. She never purposefully sent signals to any men, but they swooped down on her like birds of prey when she was in any way alone or vulnerable.

When she met Charlie Holt, he seemed different. He

was from Kansas and had come back to Iowa to visit family. He was far from refined, but impressed her with his honest talk. Built solid from toil, he nevertheless seemed gentle. He courted her like no man had ever done, taking her to church services, sitting with her on the porch. At twenty-three, he was four years older than May. He had been farming for five years in Kansas and had a sod house built there. He described the country in simple words that made her want to see it. Two weeks after she met him, they were married.

Kansas wasn't as beautiful as May had hoped, but she made a home there. About the time she started to like it, her husband went to town one night and got drunk. Over the next few months he started drinking more frequently, turning ugly when he came home.

"I don't know why I married you," he said one night. "God, if I'd known you was barren, I never would have."

May didn't understand these things, but she didn't see how she could be barren when she had been pregnant before. When she was eighteen she had suffered six weeks of sheer mortification when she became pregnant by a friend of her older brother. She never told anyone about the pregnancy or the miscarriage, adding the memories to the other ghosts that trailed her.

"Another thing," Charlie Holt added. "You tried to make me think you was a virgin, didn't you? I knowed the first night we was married you was a far sight from a virgin."

The next time Charlie came home drunk, he hit her in the face with his fist for no reason, then passed out on the bed. May had been pinned down and shoved around a couple of times, but she had never been hit. It hurt bad when Charlie hit her and made her feel like some kind of scared varmint animal in a trap.

Weeds grew up in the cornfield, and Charlie lost his draft horse in a card game. May kept a fine garden that helped to feed them, but one night Charlie poured kerosene down each row and burned it. "Teach you to mock me, goddammit, woman!" he cried, a whiskey slur stringing his words together.

May tried to stop him, but he grabbed a barrel stave and hit her with it until she was curled up on the ground whimpering.

That was all May Tremaine intended to endure. After Charlie finished his bottle and passed out, she made sure he wouldn't wake up by ringing a frying pan on the top of his head. She then packed everything she could carry and left in the middle of the night for Denver. She took her maiden name back and tried to forget she had ever been married to Charlie Holt.

She had heard that men out beyond the frontier held a higher view of the fairer sex, as women were scarce out there. Well, maybe it was true for other women, but not May. The cobbler and that man at the wagon yard had convinced her. She was doing something to provoke them. She would stop it if she knew what it was, but she didn't know. Now she was hungry and starting to think that she should use it to her advantage—whatever it was. They were going to keep coming after her, anyway. She might as well get paid for it.

Limping, she came to the house of red curtains she had seen earlier in the day. How did one apply for a job as a whore? Walk in? Maybe she should use the back door. She sat down on the front steps of the place and squinted back the tears. Maybe this was all she was good for. She had heard stories of whores marrying wealthy men out west. Maybe this was where her fortunes would change. Things couldn't get worse.

As she took off her shoes to soothe her feet, the door flew open and a cowboy staggered out, yelling as if he had a herd before him. A trail boss followed the cowboy and pushed him so hard that the cowboy tripped down the steps past May. He rolled when he hit the street and came up with his fists in front of him. Then he saw May, opened his hands, and adjusted his hat.

"Well, howdy," he said as the trail boss stepped off the stairs to the street.

May just looked away from the cowboy as she rubbed her feet gingerly.

"Where was you thirty minutes ago?" the cowboy said.

The trail boss laughed. "You mean thirty seconds."

"Hey," the young drover said, squatting in front of May, "you comin' off work or goin' on?" He grinned and put his hand on her knee.

She drew away, glancing at the boss for help, but the older man just stood staring. "I don't work here," she said. "I was just resting."

"Come on with us," the cowboy said, grabbing her wrist. "We'll go dancin' or somethin'." He stood and pulled her toward the dirt street.

She tried to wrench free, but his grip twisted her skin. "My feet hurt," she said. "I can't go."

He jerked her toward him, clamping an arm around her waist, lifting her from the steps. "I'll carry you, then. You don't even have to step on them sore feet."

The trail boss sighed. "Now, you better leave her be."

"We're dancin'," the cowboy answered.

May tried to push herself away, but the cowboy squeezed her as if he would break her back. She twisted her face away from his whiskey breath, and as she writhed in his grasp, she caught sight of a man trotting toward her on the street. A good-looking young man, well built, wearing an oilskin hunting coat.

Six

Put her down!" Clarence Philbrick said.

The cowboy looked at Clarence but kept his hold on May. "Mind your own business, son," he said, though he was not even twenty.

"I'd hate to have to whip you right here in the street," the Vermonter said, "but I will if you don't let her go." He looked at the trail boss, and the older man simply backed away a couple steps and leaned on the rail of the whorehouse porch.

The cowboy let May slide out of his grasp, and she sprang to the steps. "Stranger," the cowboy said, "if you was to try whippin' me, and I ever found out about it, I'd kick your ass all over the prairie."

Clarence cocked his arms and showed his fists. "I'll risk you finding out."

The cowboy put his hands on his hips and sized up his opponent. He looked at the trail boss.

"What are you waitin' on?" the older man said. "You been wantin' a fight all day."

The young cowboy grinned and took his coat off, throwing it aside. "Ain't you gonna get ready?"

"I believe I am ready," Clarence replied. The gold coins sewed into his sleeves were going to slow his punches somewhat, but he didn't dare take the coat off here.

"All right," the cowboy said. He raked his boot in the dirt like a bull, got wild eyed, and rushed the Vermonter, growling to the tune of ringing spurs.

Clarence stepped gracefully to one side to avoid the rush and jabbed the cowboy in the side of the jaw as he tried to swerve. The cowboy stumbled to one side and plowed headlong into the dirt.

The trail boss laughed. "Lovin' or fightin', you don't last long, do you, boy?"

The cowboy scrambled to his feet. "Stand still this time!" he ordered. He set his smarting jaw and came at Clarence again, more carefully now. Just as he drew within striking distance, he took one big step and swung the pointed toe of a boot at the Vermonter's groin.

The kick was not well disguised, but it still took Clarence off guard, and he had to hump his spine and spring backward to evade the worst. The boot caught him in the stomach, and the cowboy's fist clobbered him over the back of the head, but Clarence latched onto the leg and yanked upward with everything he had, throwing the cowboy so hard that dust flew out from under him when he hit.

The trail boss whistled a laugh up his throat and slapped his thigh.

Clarence circled and went back to his kind of fight, his fists waiting. When the cowboy sprang, he ran hard at the Vermonter, the whites of eyes and teeth showing his anger. This time Clarence used the momentum. He stood his ground, leaned into the attack, and snapped a jab into the cowboy's nose. Blood spurted as the drover stood up, and Clarence followed with a hard right that made the cowboy's knees buckle.

"All right, stranger," the trail boss said, stepping between the two. "That's enough."

Clarence stepped away and let the older man help the cowboy to his feet.

"Somebody was gonna have to do that sooner or later today," the boss said, looping the bloody cowboy's arm over his shoulder. "I'm just glad it wasn't me." He winked at Clarence, ignored May, and took the young drover away.

May buckled her shoe and stood on the steps. "Thanks," she said, looking at the ground, avoiding Clarence's eyes. She was grateful, but for all she knew, this man might treat her rougher than the cowboy.

"Don't mention it," he replied.

They stood awkwardly in silence as a steam whistle wailed far away at the depot. "My name's Clarence Philbrick," he said, thrusting his hand toward her.

"May Tremaine." She briefly touched his hand.

He took a good look at her for the first time. Her face was doll-like, blushing about the cheeks, brown eyes matching swirls of hair. He had kept in his mind, since leaving Vermont, a vague notion of courting Western women, though he knew they were few. It just went to prove his instincts. Yes, things were going to pan out here.

"Well, you can go on in now," May said, feeling uneasy under his stare.

Clarence looked at the whorehouse door and the red curtains in the window. "In there?" he said, trying to sound astounded. "You don't think . . . I was just walking back to town from camp. Just passing through this way."

"Well, so was I," she said. "My feet hurt, so I sat down here for a minute. I didn't know . . ." She made a remote gesture toward the door.

Clarence took his hat off and raked his hair back. "I

was going to have some supper," he said. "Would you think me too forward if I asked you to join me? My treat. I just got paid." He cringed inwardly. Yes, of course she'll think you're too forward. You just met her, you idiot.

May started to decline, but a hunger pang stabbed her stomach, and she got practical. "I'd like that," she said. "I don't know anybody here." She stepped down from the stairs, smiling through the torture of each stride.

They walked to a seemlier quarter of town, May trying her best to hide the limp.

"Did you get hurt back there?" Clarence asked.

"I'm wearing new shoes," she said.

In the café, they talked about where they were from, but neither cared to volunteer a reason for coming west.

May tried to remember her manners as she ate, though she was starving. "Where did you learn to fight like that?" she asked, moving her plate to cover some gravy she had slung onto the checkered tablecloth.

"I was on the boxing team in college." He chuckled. "Some of those tactics that cowboy used took me off guard. Those would have been considered poor form where I'm from." He noticed calluses on May's hands as she held a fried chicken leg daintily in her fingers.

After Clarence paid, he stood with her on the boardwalk for an awkward moment. "Can I walk you home?" he asked.

"No, thank you," she said. She had to wonder what he meant by that. He had been a perfect gentleman so far, but she had seen them blink and become predators. Still, she didn't want to part company just yet. If ever there was a time to harness that mystery that made men desire her, this seemed to be it. "Actually, I don't . . ."

Clarence waited. "Yes?" He saw that she felt uneasy and embarrassed, and the truth dawned on him. "You don't have a place to stay, do you?"

She shook her head. This was very risky. She was vulnerable now. "Don't you worry about me. I'll make out all right." She felt ridiculous. What could a college boy from Vermont possibly see in her?

"Do you have any money?"

She shook her head again.

He reached into his pocket.

"No," she said, surprising herself with the firm tone. "You've done enough for me. I won't take any more from you." She would go back to that house of red curtains before she became a beggar.

Clarence let his money drop back into his pocket and put his hand on his chin. "I can't very well leave you out here on the street."

"I'll take care of myself. You don't need to worry about me."

"Wait a minute," Clarence said. "I may have an idea. Are you determined to stay in Denver?"

She shrugged. "I don't have to stay anywhere."

"Are you religious?"

May's eyebrows pushed together, her curiosity sharpening. "I used to like to go to church. Why?"

"I hear there's a group of pilgrims camped up on Clear Creek. They're going over the mountains to establish a new town. What if we go up there and see what they're about? Maybe they'll take you in."

May tilted her head forward and looked at him. She felt the dry air parching her lips. "Pilgrims?" she said.

"It's a church. They're on a pilgrimage to find a new town site. That's all I know about them, but it wouldn't hurt to find out more, would it?"

"I guess not." It was a hope worth considering, only she didn't feel much like walking all the way up Clear Creek with her feet smarting so.

He took her by the elbow and guided her to a bench on the boardwalk. "Wait here."

"Where are you going?" she said. It felt good to get off her feet, so she sat down.

"I'll be right back." He trotted away down the street and turned a corner.

May didn't know quite what to make of Clarence Philbrick. First he wants to walk her home, then he wants to give her over to a bunch of pilgrims. She had heard about the group on Clear Creek. She read something in the paper, too. An editor had ridiculed them, calling them "cur-istians" because they allowed mingling of the races. They had even taken in a Mexican Catholic since arriving in Denver.

She sighed as a man passed her on the boardwalk, glanced up and down at her, and tipped his hat. She ignored him. Where had Clarence gone, anyway?

It was true that she had enjoyed going to church before. People were nice there. Men were on their best behavior. She liked the music, too, though she sang in such a small voice that she could scarcely hear herself. What would it be like to establish a town? A lot of hard work, probably, but she was used to that from the farm.

She had sat on the bench for several minutes when it dawned on her that maybe Clarence wasn't coming back. That was odd. He had seemed so sincere. Well, now she was on her own tonight. Her feet were too sore to walk all the way up Clear Creek to the camp-ground of the Church of the Weeping Virgin. Where was she going to sleep? God, not the wagon yard. The thought sickened her now for some reason. Dark was coming on quickly, though, and she had to think of something.

She heard a buggy whip crack and saw a nag pull a runabout around the corner. Clarence had the reins! She stood to meet him, forgetting her aching feet. He drove the horse to the edge of the boardwalk and pulled in the reins.

"Where on earth did you get that?" she said, a genuine smile showing her rows of perfect teeth.

"Hired it. Come on, let's go meet the pilgrims."

She took her skirt in her hand as she stepped into the buggy. "How much did it cost?"

"A rattletrap like this? Not enough to worry about. I didn't expect you to walk all the way up there with blisters on your feet."

He cracked the whip, and May surged ahead with the Vermonter, feeling like a gliding hawk moving effortlessly through the clapboard canyons of Denver.

Seven

It was almost dark when Dee Hassard carried his bottle from the saloon and looked at the sky. The first stars were out, wavering from his point of view, and carousers had taken over the streets. He smacked his lips and stepped down to the dirt to take his mule's reins from the rail.

"One more ride up the hill, Henrietta," he said, "then I'll be done with you." He tightened the cinch around the weary beast and mounted, holding the bottle atop his thigh like a carbine. The photographer would be long gone now, and Hassard could collect his diamond field earnings. He had had a notion about those religious fanatics earlier, but Carrol Moncrief was coming to lead them. It was better to go back east now, and let the pilgrims alone.

As he plodded toward Clear Creek, he noticed a voice filling the street somewhere ahead of him. It sounded like the rant of a hellfire and brimstone preacher, but this wasn't Sunday, and no churches stood on this street. He squinted through the twilight and located the source of the tirade.

It came from a big man in a black suit standing at the door of a saloon. The man wore a dusty hat at an angle over his forehead, a gun belt at an opposing slant across his hips. He held a Bible in one hand and a glass of whiskey in the other.

Hassard knew who it was at a glance. The resemblance to the man he had killed in South Park was unmistakable. It could be none other than the Reverend Carrol Moncrief—the Fightin' Parson.

". . . so go ahead and drink, you scoundrels!" Moncrief was saying. "By all means, drink, and I'll drink with you! Jesus loves a drunk as much as a parson. Take your toddies and your highballs, your juleps and smashes, your punches and cobblers and sours . . ."

Hassard pulled his mule up in the street, buttoned his coat to make sure Frank Moncrief's pistol and holster were covered. He put a forearm on the saddle horn and leaned into the most unusual sermon he had ever heard.

". . . but for the love of God Almighty! Don't let the devil take the stool next to you! There is a better way!"

Three men tried to enter the saloon, but the preacher stepped in the doorway.

"Sir," he said, raising his glass and singling out one of the men, "give your life to Jesus now, and I'll drink to your salvation."

The man stepped back and smirked. "Tell you what, mister. You buy me and my pals a bottle, and Jesus can share it with us." He laughed with his friends beside him.

"You can't buy your way into the Kingdom of Heaven as easy as you can buy a bottle, friend. And let me warn you: Hell is dry."

"Now, that ain't so. I've been to Dodge City, and there's liquor there to drown an army. In fact, the army drowns in it pretty regular."

The preacher shook his head slowly and began to tip the shot glass in his hand. "Your soul is poured out like this jigger," he said, watching the drink splatter on the boardwalk. He tossed the shot glass to the man. "You're empty, friend."

"What do you think we come here for?" He pushed his way past the preacher and led his group into the saloon.

"Hey!" A man in a bartender's apron stepped into the doorway and glared at the parson. "Why don't you go preach in church where you belong?"

"Anybody can preach to saints and hypocrites. I serve those who need it most: the honest sinners."

"Well, you've served here long enough. Go preach somewhere else now. You're drivin' away my customers."

"I'll stay here until I save a soul, then I'll move on," Moncrief said.

The bartender's lips curled under with frustration. "You'll move on now," he said, stepping from the saloon. He grabbed the parson by the collar.

Moncrief drew the revolver from his holster—smoothly, quickly—cocking it as its muzzle pressed against the throat of the bartender, whose eyes grew with surprise. "Don't stand between me and the work of the Lord," the parson said.

"Whoa, Preacher," the bartender wheezed. "Stay as long as you like."

"God bless you," Moncrief said, grinning as he let his pistol down. "I believe you've seen the light." He shoved the bartender back into the saloon as his eyes landed on Dee Hassard, straddling the mule in the street. "You, sir!" he cried. "I'll make you a deal for that bottle on your knee."

Hassard lifted the half-full bottle and looked at it. "What kind of deal?" He felt Lady Luck smiling on him, but this was a little spooky. Carrol so favored his dead brother that it seemed Frank was looking at him now.

The parson stepped into the street. "Throw it straight up in the air and give me one shot at it. If I miss, I'll buy you a full bottle. If I hit it, you get on your knees and give your soul over to Jesus."

Hassard looked at the bottle. "Can I take one more swig first?"

"Long as you don't swig it all," Moncrief answered.

Hassard pulled the stopper on the bottle and took a long draw. Replacing the cork, he sucked a fiery breath down his windpipe and looked at the preacher misty eyed. "Ready?" he said.

"The question is, friend, are *you* ready? You lose the bet, and Jesus wins your soul. I'll see you on your knees in this road of mud and manure if my bullet shatters that bottle."

"That'll take a miracle in this light, Preacher. Now let's see if you're really in the miracle business."

The preacher nodded, and Hassard lofted the bottle high above the false fronts of the buildings. Moncrief watched the clear glass glint in the starlight, whipped his piece from the holster, and paced the target until it reached its zenith, hanging for an instant. The Colt erupted, and glass burst from the bottle like a round of canister.

"Praise the Lord, Preacher!" Hassard dismounted as pieces of glass peppered his hat brim. When he got both feet on the ground, he stood agog and let his mouth drop open. "By golly, I feel different. I think I really do, Preacher!"

"Get down on your knees, friend. Quick, before the feelin' passes!"

Hassard pulled his hat off and dropped to his knees as if ax-handled. He went so far as to fold his hands and look up breathlessly at the preacher.

Moncrief sank to one knee beside the swindler and put his hand on Hassard's shock of red hair. "Do you renounce the devil?"

"I do!" Hassard said.

"Do you take the Lord Jesus Christ into your heart and into your life?"

"You bet!"

"Hallelujah! You can get up now."

Hassard stood and made his knees tremble. "Amen!" he shouted.

"How do you feel?" Moncrief asked.

Hassard paused and looked cockeyed at the street, as if trying to sort out some new emotion coursing through him. "I feel like I need a bath," he declared. "I'm all clean inside, and filthy on the outside."

Moncrief smiled and clapped the convert on the shoulder. "Come sit down, friend. Let's talk."

They moved together to the boardwalk and sat with their feet on the dirt street.

"Tell me," Carrol said. "How do you plan to do the work of Christ now?"

"I don't know," Hassard replied. "I've only just been saved. I reckon I don't know what I'm supposed to do. What's it like, being a Christian?"

The fighting parson breathed deep and looked at the sky. "Son, it's like all your life you've had an outlaw hoss by the tail, draggin' you around, and that tail was full of burrs. Now, all of a sudden, you just let that hoss go, and dang if it don't feel good!"

"Yeah, but the reason I was hangin' on to that hoss is 'cause I wanted to ride."

Moncrief smiled and looked his convert in the eye. What he had here was a philosopher. "You can still ride. Your new mount might seem slower than that outlaw hoss at first, but just wait till you get up to speed. This hoss has wings, son!"

"Which hoss is that, Reverend?"

"The love of the Man Upstairs, and the forgiveness of His only son, who died on the cross for you." He poked Hassard in the chest with his finger. "I know you done some bad things in your past. You ought to know what all I done before I changed hosses. But the Good Lord makes all things happen for a reason."

Hassard chuckled. "That's what I hear, but I don't

savvy much of that talk. The things I done, I don't think you'd see much reason to 'em, Preacher."

"It ain't for me to see, son. I'm just as mortal as the next man. The Good Lord sees more than you can ever wish to imagine." He rose, looking down the street for another wayward soul. "Let me warn you, friend. The devil can eat back into your heart. Bein' a Christian is hard work, but it's worth it for the way it makes you feel."

"I can do it," Hassard said. "I've been lookin' for this day. Hard to explain, but I've been searchin' for somethin', and this is it. I can feel it."

"Bless your soul," the parson said, "and go do the Lord's work in life."

Hassard shook his hand, and Moncrief turned away renewed.

"Wait, Preacher!" Hassard said. He watched the big man turn on him. "You're him, ain't you? The fightin' parson?"

"I've been called such."

"You're the Reverend Carrol Moncrief."

"I am."

Hassard curled his hat brim in his hand as he approached the preacher. "Well, Reverend Moncrief, seein' as how I'm saved now and all, I guess I might as well start the Lord's work with you. I know you're hurtin' over what happened to your brother, Frank, and I just want you to know that I feel for you, and if there's anything I can do ... Maybe say a prayer or somethin' ..."

Moncrief squinted. "What the devil are you talkin' about?"

Hassard sucked in a gasp. "Oh, Lordy, don't tell me you haven't heard. I'd have broke it easier if I thought you hadn't heard." This was so much fun that he had to fight back the smile.

"Heard what?" the preacher roared.

"Your brother's dead," Hassard said, casting his eyes to the ground.

Moncrief snorted a laugh. "You don't know Frank. He's ornerier than that."

"I know you don't want to believe it, Reverend, but I was passin' through Fairplay a while back, and I was there when they brought his body into town. They found him shot in the head somewhere out in South Park. Said he left to take some prisoner to Cañon City and never come back."

Moncrief gritted his teeth and grabbed his convert by the lapel of his dusty coat. "You better be sure of what you're sayin'." His heart felt as if it were sinking red hot into his guts.

"I wish it was somebody else tellin' you, Reverend. It ain't fair. You've just given me a new look at life, and I've got to be the one to break this news to you." He put his hand on Moncrief's fist. "Just remember, Carrol, he's gone to a better place."

The preacher opened his fist and drew away from the confidence man. "Who was the prisoner he was taking to Cañon City?"

"I couldn't tell you," Hassard said. "Didn't stay in town long enough to find out. Now, if there's anything I can do, Carrol. Anything at all . . ."

The parson pulled a watch from his pocket and turned its face to the light from the saloon. There was a train going south tonight. If he caught it he could ride to Colorado Springs, then buy a horse for the trip to Fairplay. His head was throbbing, not knowing what had happened. "I've got to get down there."

Hassard stuck his lower lip out and looked at the ground. "Well, godspeed, Carrol. I'm sure sorry you had to find out this way." He turned toward his mule.

"Wait," Moncrief said. "There is somethin' you can do."

"Name it."

"There's a bunch of pilgrims from back east camped somewhere up Clear Creek. They call theirselves the Church of the Weeping Virgin. I was supposed to meet 'em and guide 'em over the mountains. Go find 'em for me. Tell 'em they'll have to get somebody else."

Hassard smiled. "Consider it done, Carrol." He watched the reverend walk away down the street and wondered at the gullibility of man. Imagine, the likes of Dee Hassard falling for that old line of Christian nonsense. Give your life to Jesus? What in the hell did it even mean?

He was beginning to think these Moncrief brothers would fall for anything. They had gun savvy, all right. They had guts. But, for the love of God, did they trust every snake that didn't rattle?

"If there is a god," Dee Hassard said to himself, "he's smilin' on you today, boy."

Eight

❧

The runabout lurched over obstacles in the moonlit road, jostling May against Clarence from time to time on the seat. She was relieved that the Vermonter possessed the gift of conversation, or the ride up Clear Creek would have felt awkward.

They passed around a camp of men with pack saddles and strange black boxes stacked everywhere. A fine white mule caught Clarence's eye, but as the men there didn't look like pilgrims, he drove on.

When finally the campfires of the pilgrims came into view, Clarence began to feel a little uneasy. He realized that he was going to have to leave May's company here if she found the group agreeable, and he began to sense complications in his adventure. "That looks like them," he said, pointing ahead.

"My, there's a good bunch of them," May replied. She

saw some children chasing one another among the wagons.

As he drove the runabout near the camp, a man with a rifle stepped from the shadows and blocked the road.

"Whoa," Clarence said, reining in the livery horse.

"Who are you?" the guard demanded, holding his weapon ready in front of him.

"I'm Clarence Philbrick. This is Miss May Tremaine. We'd like to speak with the leader of your group."

"You want to join us?"

"We just want to ask some questions right now."

"You got guns?" the man said.

"Not on me," Clarence answered.

"Get out of the buggy and walk up," the guard ordered.

Clarence looked at May. Neither felt eager to get out of the vehicle under the circumstances.

"Ain't no harm gonna come to you," the guard said. "We got to be careful, that's all. Been attacked in some places."

Clarence looked for May's approval.

She shrugged. "We came this far. We might as well talk to them."

As the guard escorted them toward the camp, May noticed something odd about the circle of people around the nearest fire. It first struck her as a writhing. Every hand was busy working on something. One man was oiling harnesses. Another was braiding a bullwhacker's whip. A woman bounced a baby on her knee as she mended a quilt. There were faces of all colors, some ruddy, some pale, some dark.

Clarence noticed an Indian woman, her hair long and straight, parted in the middle. A necklace of teeth and claws lay across the bodice of her faded print dress.

Next to her sat a black man who was whittling a walking stick. He had to be six-foot-six and couldn't weigh more than a hundred fifty. The man sat on a stool with his legs crossed, yet both feet lay flat on the ground. He looked up as the arrivals came near, and Clarence found a full head of gray hair and a large white mustache contrasting with his dark brown skin, a twinkle in his eyes struggling through reflections on his spectacles. He stood. "Is this him?" he said to the guard.

"Nope," the guard answered.

"You were expecting somebody else?" Clarence said.

"A Reverend Moncrief was supposed to meet us here tonight. He's to guide us over the mountains. But that's not for you to worry about. I'm Elder Hopewell. What can we do for you?"

Clarence saw a bunch of children spying on him from under a wagon. "Miss Tremaine would like to know a little about your group. She's all alone and looking for a place to settle out here."

"What would you like to know?" Hopewell said.

May swept her eyes across the faces peering up at her. "This is a Christian church, isn't it?"

The group around the fire raised a round of low laughter.

"We are *the* Christian church," Elder Hopewell replied, his teeth showing under the full white mustache. "All others have fallen into disfavor with the Maker and will have to be reconciled."

"According to what authority?" Clarence said.

"According to the Holy Virgin."

"Has she told you so?"

"Not me," Elder Hopewell explained. "The late Pastor Wyckoff received the visitations. It started seven years ago in Philadelphia. The Angel of Mary came to him in the night as he prayed. She was crying over the sad state of humanity, especially those who call themselves Christians yet obey the wicked laws of government and materialism over the laws of God. The Weeping Virgin told Pastor Wyckoff to gather the downtrodden faithful among the many races and repair to a new promised land. We are the New Order that will bring all the peoples of the world together."

"Amen," someone in the circle said. They had all

nodded as Elder Hopewell told the story, their hands remaining busy with their tasks.

"Now, if you want to travel with us," Hopewell said, "we'd be happy to take you in. But if you want to truly join us, you have to give all your material possessions to the church."

"I don't have any material possessions," May said.

"Will you give your service to the church?"

May's eyes shifted. "What kind of service?"

The elder pointed to the people around the fire. "Like these folks are doing. Fix what needs to be fixed. Build what needs building. Everything we do is for the good of the church, and no time is spent idle."

"I don't mind work," May said.

"You'll have to read Pastor Wyckoff's book," Hopewell said. "And when you're ready, you will renounce all other authority and become a vested member of the Church of the Weeping Virgin. Until that time, you are welcome to share our company, our food, and our friendship." He looked at Clarence. "What about you, young man? Will you come with us, too?"

Clarence shook his head. "I have business in New Mexico." He took May by the arm. "Will you excuse us a minute?" He pulled her a few yards away from the circle of pilgrims. "I don't know if this is such a good idea," he said.

"They seem like nice folks," she replied.

"What about this business of the visitations and all? Sounds a little strange to me."

"Yes, but that was their pastor, and he's dead. These people look all right."

Clarence glanced over May's shoulder at the congregation, then looked back down at her face. She was looking up at him, as if waiting for his approval. He could see that she was going to go with them. She had nowhere else to turn. She couldn't go with him to New Mexico, could she? No, of course not. What choice did she have? She was going to join these pilgrims. He could leave her with doubts and misgivings, or he could bolster her confidence.

"I believe you're right," he said. "They seem like nice people, and there are enough of them to offer protection. You'll be all right with them."

May smiled again, her eyes twinkling gratefully. "Thank you for everything you've done. I won't forget you."

Clarence shuffled his feet. "When you get settled, I want you to write me a letter. Send it general delivery to Santa Fe. Let me know where you've settled so I can come check up on you someday."

She looked away, her face flushing. She began to speak, but a rattle of rocks across the creek interrupted her.

A mule splashed through the shallow stream and into the firelight as the guard stepped forward to challenge the rider.

"Howdy, brothers and sisters in Christ!" a red-haired man shouted from the back of the mule.

"Who are you?" the guard demanded.

"Put your weapon away, friend. I'm your guide. I'm to take you over the mountains."

Elder Hopewell approached the stranger and stood beside the camp guard. "You're Reverend Moncrief?"

"The good reverend couldn't make it. His brother's been murdered in South Park. He sent me in his stead. I'm Deacon Dee Hassard." He got down from the mule and held a hand out to the elder.

"When will Reverend Moncrief join us?" Hopewell asked.

"I have a feelin' he'll be huntin' his brother's murderer for a spell. You'll have to make do with me. He had to go to Fairplay while the trail was still hot." He looked past Hopewell at the crowd around the nearest campfire. "Carrol didn't have much time to fill me in. How many people have you got here?"

"Almost two hundred, counting the children."

"And about the money. Five hundred?"

"We have it, as we promised."

"No offense, but I'd like to see it."

Elder Hopewell motioned for Hassard to follow and led the new arrival to the tailgate of a broken-down wagon. He pulled a pair of saddlebags out and opened one flap.

Hassard craned his neck to see by the light of a lantern hanging from a cottonwood limb above. When the elder pulled a roll of bills out and handed it over, Hassard glimpsed more currency deeper in the pouch. He saw the glint of gold and silver coins, heard them chink. Glorious thoughts of larceny rushed by like ripples in the nearby creek.

"Carrol said you'd be ready to go." Hassard slipped the roll of bills into his pocket.

"We are," the elder replied.

Hassard snorted. "Not with these wagons." He approached the pilgrims around the nearest fire. "Friends, we've got work to do, and we'd best get started right now if we want to leave tomorrow. First thing we do is load the wagons with anything that won't travel on a pack mule. We'll drive into Denver at daybreak and sell the wagons and everything in 'em."

"Now hold on there, Deacon," the elder said. "We've got household items in there. Tables, chairs, beds. Things of necessity."

Hassard twisted his face. "I thought you folks wanted to go across the divide to the Promised Land."

"And we will," the tall man said.

"Elder Hopewell, there are no roads where we're goin'. Wagons won't make it. It's best to convert all those material possessions to cash. Better yet—gold. Your church can use it to pay homestead fees or buy government land. Besides, it's a land of milk and honey over there, brothers and sisters." He turned to the people in the camp, speaking loudly. "You can build your own household goods from the bounty of God's green earth!"

"You've been to the Western slopes?" Elder Hopewell asked.

"I have, brother, and it is the most beautiful spot in the world. But gettin' there's gonna test your faith, and we've got to get started as soon as practical."

The elder caught some of Dee Hassard's false enthusiasm and smiled back at the congregation. "What do we do?" he asked.

"Get those wagons loaded with everything we don't need," Hassard cried. "Keep only your clothes, your weapons, and your tools. We'll sell everything else in Denver tomorrow and start west."

Elder Hopewell raised his hands, reaching high in the air. "It's time," he said. This was a relief. They had been waiting here too long, and everyone had looked to him since Pastor Wyckoff's murder. Now there was someone here who knew where to go. "Let's get ready!"

The people rose as if bolting from Sunday services.

"One more thing," Hassard shouted. "Remember Reverend Moncrief in your prayers tonight! His brother's been murdered."

"Amen!" someone shouted, and the camp surged for the wagons to separate everything that wouldn't fit a pack saddle.

"I think I better go help them," May said. She and Clarence had watched the arrival of Deacon Hassard in silence.

"Good luck," Clarence said, taking her hand, releasing it reluctantly.

She joined the pilgrims, and he turned to the rented buggy. It didn't feel right leaving her there. It wasn't that she was in any danger. No, it was something else. He was going to miss her. He had only known her a couple of hours, yet he already regretted parting ways with her.

As Clarence Philbrick drove through the night back to Denver, he began to wonder what lay waiting for him in New Mexico. Was the Ojo de los Brazos as easy to look at as May Tremaine? Would it be worth the journey?

He began to compose his nightly journal entry:

> *I once went hunting for ducks and killed the largest brace of grouse I had ever bagged. I arrived at my duck blind very late, yet found fine sport there as well.*
>
> *Is May Tremaine a bird of serendipity—a pleasant diversion along my way to fortune? Or is she a siren who tempts me to stray from my course, onto the rocks of ruin?*

Nine

It was an embarrassment. Ramon del Bosque could still hear the jeers of his friends, even though he was a long day's journey from Guajolote.

"Adios, Padre Ramon," they had said, taunting him as he left the village, leading Sister Petra's burro. One of them had run into the street to give Ramon a whip made of yucca fibers so he could flagellate himself like the *penitentes*.

"What do you have that *disciplina* for?" Petra had asked.

"For the burro," Ramon had said, striking the animal a light blow across the rump with the whip.

It was bad enough that Ramon's father was always saying he was going to send Ramon to the school in Santa Fe to become a priest. That claim had caused Ramon no end of consternation: his friends constantly coming to him for confessions and calling him "Padre

Ramon." But this was a humiliation almost too severe to endure.

God had spoken to Sister Petra. At least, that was what Sister Petra claimed. She had been praying nine days, not getting enough food or rest. She had fainted in her room and had had a dream. That was all. It was her own mind, not God, that had said, "The cross awaits you on the mountainside."

Ramon thought he must be the only one in Guajolote to remember that Sister Petra was, after all, an Anglo. Yes, she spoke Spanish perfectly, but she had green eyes, for heaven's sake. Why was this crazy Anglo to be taken so seriously? She was not going to save Guajolote. The Anglos were going to get it, and people were going to be thrown out of their homes. Why was he the only one who could see that?

Sister Petra's claim had thrown Guajolote into turmoil, and no one had gotten more excited than Ramon's father. "I will send Ramon with you to find the cross on the mountain!" he had blurted. "Ramon is going to be a priest, you know. He will be your disciple, Sister Petra! You can use my burro!"

Now he was farther from home than he had ever been—a day's walk north, approaching the village of Chacon. Sister Petra had interpreted her dream to mean that she was to go to one of the hills on which the *penitentes* held their mock crucifixions every Easter. The nearest *penitente* chapter was in Chacon, and so that was where Sister Petra had decided to begin her search.

As he got his first glimpse of the village, Ramon simply could not take the pace any longer. "Sister Petra," he said. "Can we slow down now? We are almost there."

She was several steps ahead of Ramon and the burro, and she stopped to let them catch up, glaring at him with those green Anglo eyes. "You have been complaining since the moment we started yesterday," she snapped.

"But I have a cramp right here," he said, putting a hand over his stomach.

"You shouldn't have eaten so much breakfast this morning. You knew we were going to have to walk."

"We haven't been walking. We've been trotting like coyotes."

"How old are you?"

"Fourteen."

"I am more than twice your age. You should be able to keep up with me."

"I can keep up with you. I just don't want to."

Petra put her hands on her hips and scowled. "You don't believe in what I'm doing, do you?"

"No. What do you think you're going to find when you get to this cross on this mountain?"

"I don't know. I just know that God has instructed me to find it."

Ramon scoffed and rolled his eyes.

"If you prefer, I can send you back to Guajolote right now," Petra warned. "You've only been slowing me down."

The thought of returning in ridicule quickly sobered Ramon. His father would not be happy, and his friends would heckle him for days. It was better to let the excitement die down and return in a week or so. "All right, I'm sorry," he said.

"Throw that *disciplina* away," Petra ordered. "Juan will think you have it to make fun of him."

They proceeded into the village, Petra going directly to the shop of Juan Hidalgo, the carpenter in Chacon, and the *hermano mayor* of the *penitentes* there.

"Hello, Brother Juan," she said, finding him around the back of his shop.

Juan stopped sawing the cottonwood beam he was fashioning into an axle for his *carreta* and looked over his shoulder. "Sister Petra!" he said, his eyebrows gathering droplets of sweat into the creases of his forehead. He lay his saw down and came forward to take Petra's hand in his. Sawdust clung to his hands and his sleeves, and he dropped to one knee and bowed before the sister. "What brings you to Chacon?" he asked.

"I have prayed a novena to save our village," Petra said, "and God spoke to me."

Juan gasped and seemed so excited that he didn't even notice young Ramon del Bosque leading the burro around the corner of the adobe. "What did God say to you?"

"He said, 'The cross awaits you on the mountainside.' "

Juan touched the points of the cross on his forehead and body. "Do you think the cross on the mountain means our *Calvario* where we stand the cross during Holy Week?"

"I don't know," she said. "I am just beginning my search."

Juan nodded, smiling at the boy with the burro. "Who is this young fellow with you?"

Petra fought the urge to tell Juan that this young fellow was a pain in the neck sent by God to test her. "This is Ramon. His father sent him to help me search."

The carpenter put his hand on the boy's shoulder. "You should be proud. Not every young boy like you gets to go on such an adventure. I only wish I could go with you, but I have the people to take care of here."

Ramon drew away uncertainly from the carpenter. In Guajolote there were no *penitentes*, and he only knew what he had heard. He knew it was true that during most of the year, the brotherhoods accomplished charity works in their villages, helping those in need, counseling those who suffered. They lived normal lives, doing Christian works.

But during Holy Week, the *penitentes* would allow a *sangrador* to cut slashes across their backs with a knife. They would whip themselves with the *disciplina* made of yucca fibers, causing blood to flow from the knife wounds. On Good Friday, some of them would carry huge wooden crosses to the *Calvario*. And, every year, one would be chosen to crucify. His brothers would tie him to a cross and raise it into place, leaving him there until he lost consciousness. Ramon had even heard that some of the *penitente* chapters used real nails instead of rope, and that some men had died on the cross.

He looked at the hand on his shoulder and didn't see any nail scars through the sawdust but still felt uneasy enough to pull away.

"Which is the hill that your *morada* uses as its *Calvario*?" Sister Petra asked. She was anxious to see her quest through, to save her village, and to please her god.

Juan turned on Ramon and glared at him. "I will take you to it, but you—young man—you must promise never to tell anyone which hill we use. It is getting harder for us to keep outsiders away. They want to come and watch us perform the penance—especially the *Americanos*. They think we are some sort of *locos*."

"He won't tell anybody," Sister Petra promised. "I will make sure of that."

Ramon resented Petra's speaking for him, and he smirked at her. "I won't tell," he said to the carpenter.

They tied the burro at a water trough made of a hollowed-out log and followed a well-worn trail into the foothills. Sister Petra seemed excited, walking faster than ever. The carpenter matched her pace, and Ramon lagged only a few strides behind. He might have stayed in Chacon with the burro, but he was curious about the *Calvario*, where men hung from crosses. Perhaps the story of it would silence the jeers of his friends for a while when he got back to Guajolote.

"This is the place," Juan Hidalgo said, gesturing to the hill.

Petra paused at the bottom to catch her breath, then scrambled up the trail to the summit. When Ramon reached the top of the little mountain, he found the nun on her knees. He turned away from her and looked back toward Chacon. He couldn't see the village. The *Cal-*

vario was secluded, so that the ritual might remain hidden from outsiders.

Mopping his sleeve across his brow, he searched the ground for signs of blood, maybe a nail or a crown of thorns or something. He felt the carpenter looking at him and met the pleasant gaze of Juan Hidalgo. The *penitente* motioned toward a small piñon tree near the summit, and Ramon joined him in its shadow, sitting side by side on the shaded rocks. They waited in silence only a couple of minutes, then heard Petra shuffling through the gravel.

"This is not the place," the nun said.

Juan rose from the shade of the scrubby tree, obviously disappointed. "Are you sure? If you want, I will build a cross and get the brothers to help me raise it here. Didn't the voice of God tell you to seek the cross?"

"It wouldn't do any good," Petra said. She sighed and looked northward. "This is not the place."

Juan felt deeply disappointed. "Where will you go now?"

"To the north," Petra said. "I feel that is the way to go. I feel the mountain is higher. I will search among the brotherhoods farther north, and higher up. I think that is what God wants me to do."

Ramon scrambled to his feet and stared at the nun. "But how far are you going?" he asked. "How long is this going to take?"

She shrugged. "Who can say? You can go back home if you want to, Ramon. But I am going to take your father's burro with me." She walked past the carpenter and tramped down the trail back toward the village.

Juan chuckled. "You should go with her, Ramon. She is going to go high up into the mountains where it will be cool. I bet you are going to see a lot of new things you have never seen before. It will be an adventure to shape the rest of your life."

Ramon shook his head and looked up at the rising flanks of the Sangre de Cristos. "She thinks she is going to keep the Ojo de los Brazos grant from being sold," he said. "I don't know what she expects to find up there."

"God speaks to her. I believe it. She might need you, Ramon. Are you going to go with her?"

Ramon shrugged, his shoulders pushing out a sigh as they fell. "I guess so. A little farther, anyway."

The carpenter slapped the boy on the back. "You are going to see something wonderful, Ramon. Now hurry up before she leaves without you."

Ten

❧

Clarence could hear his father talking: "Good God, boy! If I'd have been as naive as you in California . . . irresponsible is what it is . . . most foolhardy thing I ever heard of . . ." The old forty-niner would have lectured for hours.

But as Clarence stared at the Denver and Rio Grande schedule posted in the depot, he knew he was not going to buy a ticket. He was not going to ride the rails south, toward New Mexico and the Ojo de los Brazos grant. He still intended to get there sooner or later, but it didn't feel right going just now. Not with May Tremaine taking a different trail west. And, anyway, Clarence's father wasn't looking over his shoulder here. He could do anything he wanted.

He had seen Deacon Dee Hassard and several of the men from the pilgrim camp hawking wagon loads of goods early this morning. They had sold everything, bought burros and pack saddles, and trailed out of town. They were taking the road into the mountains, pushing toward the mining camps, and ultimately into unsettled lands.

Clarence didn't care what his father would say. All he knew was that he had left May too hastily. Some people called them fanatics, after all. He was responsible for whatever happened to her while she was with them. He had to be sure.

He gripped the Remington rifle by the octagonal barrel, resting the breech across his shoulder. Stooping, he grabbed his traveling bag and marched out of the depot. He felt like he ought to run in order to catch up, but he settled for a fast walk. By the time he reached the edge of town, he was only slightly winded, and just getting his legs warmed up.

The grade started to pitch uphill along Clear Creek, but Clarence only strode longer. He stopped when he reached the former campground of the Church of the Weeping Virgin, took off his heavy coat, and put it in his bag.

Only ashes shifted where last night the pilgrims had sat mending and making things. The silence and emptiness made the Vermonter anxious to catch up, so he picked up his things and stepped briskly up the path.

The trail veered onto the Georgetown Road. Clarence could see footprints and burro tracks in the dirt. He figured he would catch them in camp at Golden. They wouldn't try to get too far the first day.

He climbed as the day warmed, stopping occasionally to look eastward, across the plains. He had hunted the Eastern mountains, taken in the scenery from various promontories. But this vista was unlike anything he had ever seen. The country was so big here, the view so long through the thin air. A body could see miles and miles of wide-open range, nothing like the shrinking pockets of dark forest wilderness back east.

Two days ago he had been a buffalo skinner in a treeless infinity of rolling grass. Now he was climbing ever higher among scattered pines and rocky passes. If he had known about this place, he would have come long ago, with or without his damned trust fund. The air here was so fine that a body could almost live on it like fuel.

When he approached Golden in the early afternoon, he sensed clouds gathering in the pass. By the time he reached the town, rain was falling in sheets. He took refuge in a wagon-yard barn and ate some grub he had packed for the day's hike.

"Goin' prospectin'?" the man in the barn asked, himself taking a break from the weather.

"No," Clarence answered. "I'm trying to catch up to a party of pilgrims. I'm going to help guide them across the mountains."

"They passed through town a couple of hours ago. Their guide traded mules with me. Said they was gonna try to get to Idaho Springs today."

"How far is that?" Clarence asked, holding his tin cup in the rain to collect some water.

"Better part of twenty miles."

Clarence's eyes bulged as he turned to the stable man. "That far?"

"That guide was hell-bent on coverin' some ground today."

The Vermonter stood immediately, put on his hat, and buttoned the oilskin coat harboring his fortune. "I'd better cover some myself then." He picked up his Remington and stepped toward the downpour cascading from the eaves of the barn. "You wouldn't have a ten-dollar horse for sale, would you?" he said, thinking of the miles that lay ahead.

"Got a three-year-old. Last year's bronc. He's gentled down right nice since we cut him. You won't get him for ten dollars, though."

All Clarence could think of, as he rode his new twelve-dollar mount up the slippery road, was poor May's feet. How was she going to walk twenty miles today with those blisters? He only hoped they would let her ride a burro part of the way, otherwise she would be miserable. She didn't even have a slicker to turn the rain.

The road continued to climb, and Clarence noticed that his gelding had a bad habit of tossing his head. He could fix that with a piece of rope tied between saddle girth and headstall, but he didn't have a piece of rope just now. The pilgrims would, he thought.

The rain stopped, clouds broke, and shafts of sunlight began to light circles on the mountainsides. He reached the edge of a mountain forest and stopped for one last look across the plains, sensing that the great ranges were about to engulf him.

After a couple of hours, the tracks of the pilgrims became clearer in the muddy road and Clarence knew they had passed here after the rain. He didn't see many small tracks and figured the children had given out and were either riding burros or their parents' backs.

He was having misgivings again. What business of his was the life of May Tremaine? Here he was carrying a fortune in gold into a wilderness. Perhaps he should have put it in a bank back in Denver, for safekeeping until he decided to head south. Too late now. The plan that had seemed so clear when he left Vermont was starting to break apart like melting ice on a river. If he lost that gold, his father would never let him forget it.

He stopped on a hill and saw several trails of smoke below where miners had carved a town into the valley. This had to be Idaho Springs. The near slopes stood divested of timber, which had been made into buildings for the ungainly town. He could see rude log cabins ringing the settlement, a few painted Victorians in one quarter bespeaking mineral wealth.

He wondered if the Ojo de los Brazos would look the way this place had before the mines—the high rocky peaks cradling forests and green valleys. He hoped so. He could imagine driving May up to the gate in a carriage on a sunny day.

What was he thinking? He barely knew this woman.

Clarence swung down from his horse and squatted at the side of the road. The cheap saddle he had bought was going to make him sore if he didn't walk the rest of the way. He put his rifle butt on the ground and gripped the barrel to steady himself as he balanced on the balls of his feet. What if New Mexico didn't look like this? What if May had no intention of going with him there? What would he do then? Give his earthly possessions to the Church of the Weeping Virgin? Become a religious fanatic?

Maybe he should have bought that train ticket this morning. He could have been in Pueblo by now. Well, no choice but to find the pilgrims and go over the mountains with them at this point. Come on, Clarence, you've got to see something through.

He led his horse into Idaho Springs and found out that the pilgrims were camped just up the creek from town. He was hoping they would give him food and take him in when he got there, but he knew no guarantees.

The burro tracks took him to the edge of the stream, where he found the pilgrims engaged in various forms of industry, though with little spring left to step with.

"Howdy," a guard said when he saw Clarence approach camp. "Good to see you again."

"Look!" someone else shouted. "It's Sister May's friend!"

Clarence took his bag down from the saddle horn and stared with wonder at the people stepping forward to greet him. May's friend? It was as if she had been among them for years.

"She told us how you helped her out in Denver," a woman from Pennsylvania said. "God bless you, Clarence."

He spotted Deacon Dee Hassard sitting against a tree trunk with a book in his hand. The pathfinder sprang to his feet and came toward him.

"May!" someone was shouting. "Clarence is back!"

"What brings you back?" Hassard said, smiling as he offered his hand.

"Thought I might help you take these folks over the mountains," Clarence said, pulling his coat from the loop handles of his traveling bag before someone picked it up and felt its heft.

"What for?"

Clarence shrugged. "Never been over the mountains before. Thought I could help these people get there, see some new country."

"Well, you've got a good rifle," Hassard said. "How would you like to scout ahead and hunt for meat?"

Clarence fought the smile back. "All right." He noticed a teenage girl leading May up from the creek.

"Elder Hopewell!" Hassard cried. "Get another copy of Pastor Wyckoff's book for Brother Clarence, if you please." He turned back to the Vermonter and shook the open book in his face. "You've got to read this," he said. "It'll open your eyes," and he turned back toward his tree to continue reading.

The girl led May to Clarence and turned away, giggling. The other pilgrims smiled coyly and went back to their chores, leaving the couple alone at the edge of camp.

"They do make a fuss, don't they?" May said, blushing.

Clarence nodded. "It's welcome after that long walk. How did your feet hold out today?"

May smiled and stuck a toe out from under her hem. "That Comanche woman—her name is Mary Whitepath—she gave me these moccasins. They don't hurt at all."

Elder Hopewell approached the couple on his gangling legs and towered above them. "Here's your book, Brother Clarence."

"I'm not sayin' I want to join your church," Clarence explained. "Just thought I might see some new country with you and help you find a place to settle."

"Will you read the book?"

"I don't see any harm in that."

"That's all we ask. I hope you will learn to walk in the way that leads to light." Elder Hopewell gave him the book and turned back toward camp.

"I've been readin' that book," May said. "Some of it's all right, but other parts . . ."

"What?"

"It's just hard to believe."

Clarence raised his eyebrows and looked across the campground at the busy pilgrims. "Did you ever expect you'd fall in with a bunch like this?"

"I didn't know there was such a bunch as this."

They stood looking at each other—the Vermonter and the runaway wife—neither feeling quite awkward enough to break the stare.

Eleven

❧

The eyes were wide open under Dee Hassard's hat. His head lay on a packsaddle, the edge of a blanket curled under his chin. Pastor Wyckoff's book, *The Wisdom of Ages*, lay open on his chest, and one hand rested across its spine. His lungs drew deep, as if he had fallen into the rhythm of sound sleep, but his mind was conscious, plotting, rehearsing.

The late Pastor Wyckoff was a genius, he was thinking. Hassard only wished he had thought of the scam himself. To an eye honed for deception, it was all laid out like a thinly disguised recipe for fraud in *The Wisdom of Ages*.

He held a reverent smile under his brim as he walked mentally through the formula again. Wyckoff's first step: he makes himself a pastor—the easy way. Creates his own religion. No Bible lessons, no seminary.

Only in America.

Hassard couldn't imagine why he hadn't seen it before, but religious freedom had opportunity written all over it. You conjure a revelation, proclaim yourself a prophet—bang, you're in business.

According to *The Wisdom of Ages*, Wyckoff's revelation arrives in the image of the Virgin Mary. She appears weeping over his bed one night, lamenting the sorry state of the wicked world. She tells Wyckoff to gather the poor downtrodden faithful from all the races and start over. Presto, there's your congregation.

It helps to be a good writer, Hassard thought. That Wyckoff could really mold the lingo, yet *The Wisdom of Ages* read like a dime novel, in simple language, with its philosophies easily understood. There was a reason for that. The book was designed to appeal to the poorly educated.

This part is hard to figure, Hassard thought. Wyckoff goes after poor people with little schooling. Where's the logic in that? Poor folks have no money to steal. It makes no sense at first. But that's why it's good—it's hard to figure.

Wyckoff isn't after just any poor folks. He wants honest, hardworking, trusting Christian souls—"the generous poor" as he calls them in his book. They don't have money to take, but they'll work. What a thrust! Didn't the Virgin Mary tell Wyckoff in his vision that all members of the New Order must work every waking moment to keep the devil from infesting their souls? No hand was ever to lie idle for even an instant.

Hassard could hardly stay still thinking of it. Take the church's built-in tenet for constant work, and add to it the Virgin Mary's order that every member give every penny earned to the church, and you have an organization that can only get richer. Wyckoff sits back and counts money while his new recruits keep chipping in their meager earnings.

Next step, publicity. Distribute the book, give a few sermons, convert a few souls. Let it build. Wyckoff is bound to run into opposition, of course. He's telling everyone to renounce money, government, and all other symbols of man's authority—especially other religions. He goes so far as to claim that the Bible is incomplete without *The Wisdom of Ages*. His is the only true Christianity.

But the preachers and priests and parsons won't stand for some upstart prophet shaving off pieces of their pie. They condemn Wyckoff, stir the resentment against him, foment the festering hatreds. They all but condone acts of violence and vandalism perpetrated against the Church of the Weeping Virgin and its members.

So what does Wyckoff do? He takes it like a true martyr for a while, raking in sympathy and new members. Religious fanatics feed off of persecution. It pulls them closer together. Then, when things get really bad, Wyckoff heads west, to new country, where no clergy rule. There his church will work for him, make him wealthy, carve his domain.

But he makes a fatal mistake. On the way west, Wyckoff probes the Old South for converts. Hassard rocked his head on the pack saddle at the folly of it. Wyckoff has grown too cocky at this point. He's been lucky so far, and now he's pushing it. Some white folks in Arkansas take issue with Wyckoff's marrying colored to whites, and they lynch him. You don't mess around with those Southern boys.

The mixing of the races is not a bad idea by itself. It excludes no one, appeals to immigrants. And people who will stand for it don't hate anybody. They're harmless. But Wyckoff should have been smart enough to know it would never go over in the South. Audacity has to be reined in somewhere.

Now he's a poor, dead, fake martyr. He could have had his own kingdom out here. And if Carrol Moncrief wasn't coming back after my hide, Hassard thought, I could pick it up where Wyckoff dropped it. As it lies, I can only take the Church of the Weeping Virgin for what it's worth now, and it doesn't have over a thousand dollars in its coffers.

The swindler shifted on a rock that was poking up into his back. The important thing, he had decided, was knowing the strategy of the scam, and there was still one aspect of the church he hadn't been made privy to: the initiation.

This was something they only whispered about, but he had gathered a little. When a new recruit had read *The Wisdom of Ages* and had decided to join the church, several of the congregation members would put the recruit through a three-day initiation process of some kind. Browbeating and lecturing, Hassard suspected. Whatever it was, it worked. Weeping Virginites were loyal to excess and kept the initiation rites a secret.

Anyway, once he figured out how to conduct the initiation, he could swindle the pilgrims, stay one step ahead of Moncrief, and go somewhere else to put his own twists on Wyckoff's grand swindle—maybe Canada or Australia.

Earlier today he had thought about just grabbing the money and making a run for it in the night. Then that greenhorn from back east showed up—Clarence what's-his-name. He looked just brave and dumb enough to give chase. Hassard had heard May Tremaine tell how Clarence had fought off the cowboy in Denver for her. All he needed was a college boy putting practical thoughts into the heads of his pilgrims. That was why he had made the Vermonter a hunter. To keep him away from the congregation.

Keep him away from Sister May, too. Dee Hassard knew that look. She was no weeping virgin. That gal had used what God gave her to get by before. Now that Clarence had come back, it looked as if he was going to have to string this thing out a little longer than he had at first planned. That was all right. Maybe he would find time to discover the secrets of the initiation rites and have a religious experience with Sister May.

He snorted, forcing her out of his thoughts. The cold mountain air streamed under the hat, into his nostrils. He heard Clear Creek boiling among its time-rounded boulders, the wind rattling twigs against the starry sky. The time was right. Dee Hassard was about to show the ghost of Pastor Wyckoff a thing or two about audacity.

He bolstered his gall, chose his opening line. Coiling his resolve like a twisted spring, he held a breath and waited for the release.

"Great God!" he shouted, springing up from the ground. He threw the blanket aside, staggered, and fell across the gangling legs of Elder Hopewell. "Wake up, everybody!"

The elder flinched as he woke and scrambled out from under Hassard. "What is it?" he said, groping for his sensibilities.

"It's a wonder!" Hassard shouted. He pulled his knees under him, clasped his hands, and made out like he was searching the heavens.

One of the pilgrims rose a short distance away. "Everything all right?"

"Yes," Hassard moaned. "It's wonderful."

"What's got into you?" Elder Hopewell said.

Hassard jumped to his feet. "Everybody, wake up!" he shouted, waving his arms. "I know what to do now!"

Voices began to mutter and pilgrims sat up in their blankets. A few of the more curious came trotting to Elder Hopewell's fire, and Clarence Philbrick arrived in stocking feet with his Remington rifle in one hand and his coat under his arm.

"Settle down," Hopewell said, putting his hand on Hassard's shoulder. "Tell us what you're talking about."

Hassard had made his eyes moist and used them now to catch the moonlight as he stared up at the elder. "I was meditating on Pastor Wyckoff's book," he said, his voice shaking. "I sank into a deep state, like nothing I ever felt before. And *she came to me*!"

"Who?" someone said, pushing into the circle that had formed around Hassard.

"Just like the book said. It was the Weeping Virgin! She told me where to lead the faithful!"

Clarence put the butt of the rifle on the ground and searched for May, finding her approaching the ring of pilgrims to his left.

"Are you sure you weren't just dreaming?" Elder Hopewell said.

"Dreamin'!" Hassard said, glaring up at the tall man. "No dream feels like that. I'm tellin' you, the Virgin spoke to me! She told me where to lead this church!"

"Well, where?" asked a man in the crowd. "Where are we going?"

Hassard wheeled slowly and looked at his listeners, raising his hands slowly. "There's a peak high up in the Sawatch," he said. "I've heard of it before. Thought it was only a legend. But the Virgin Mary told me for sure, and now I know. It's there, and that's where she wants us to go."

"What peak?" Clarence asked.

"I've heard of mountain men and prospectors seein' it," Hassard said, building on the curiosity around him. "Never met anybody who actually found it. It lies against the wall of a high basin above the timberline. The basin is small—just a few miles across, I guess. You can only see it from a few places along the north rim."

"See *what*?" Clarence demanded.

The swindler imagined the lucre he would win as Pastor Dee Hassard, and let the light of wonder fill his eyes. "The cross," he whispered. "A giant cross of pure snow driven into the crevices of the mountainside. I've heard it's a thousand feet tall, three hundred wide, with arms lifting toward heaven." He flattened his palms and spread his arms, turning in the circle of pilgrims, relishing the looks of stupor on their faces. Then his eyes crossed the skeptical glare of that damned Vermonter. "It's the Mount of the Snowy Cross."

"If you've never seen it, how do you know what it looks like?" Clarence asked.

"The revelation, boy! The Weeping Virgin! She's seen it!" He stepped toward the west curve of the circle around him and walked a few steps into the congregation, the pilgrims making way for him. Suddenly he pointed over their heads. "It's that way!" he cried. "That's the way we're to go."

Clarence smirked. "That's the way we've *been* going."

Hassard wheeled, spread his arms, smiled. "Now we know why."

The pilgrims began to mumble, and Elder Hopewell spoke above them. "All right, let's go back to bed," he said, calming the people with strokes of his long fingers over their heads. "We've got to rise early."

"As Elder Hopewell says," Hassard agreed. "We've got another long day's march ahead of us." He picked up his blanket and his book and went back to his packsaddle, lying back against it as the pilgrims dispersed.

He could tell by the looks on their faces that he had hooked them. Elder Hopewell was a little skeptical yet, but he would come around. The problem, if there was going to be one, would come from Clarence what's-his-name.

He rolled onto his side as he pulled the blanket up to his chin. Looking across the campground, he watched the pilgrims shuffling back toward their beds. And there was Clarence—talking with Sister May. He was swaying her, too. Look at her, peering up at him, hanging on his every word. What a form she cut in the moonlight! Young Clarence was going to require special treatment. And so was Sister May.

Twelve

It was an ugly hump in the ground—fresh dirt sculpted by a recent rainfall. Carrol Moncrief compared it to the surrounding plots in the young Fairplay cemetery. Most of them were grass covered, and flat or concave. Frank's was mounded high, bare of vegetation, sun cracked.

He had never thought about the life of a grave before, but it was suddenly obvious. The pine box buried below him would someday rot and collapse. This mound of dirt would fall in on his brother. The ground would sink, collect water instead of shed it, and grass would sprout.

The marker at the head of the mound was just a wooden cross with Frank's name carved on it. Carrol figured the county would put up a good stone one, seeing as how Frank had been sheriff.

His horse, tied behind him at the fence of pine pickets, jingled the bridle and stomped a foot, fighting off flies.

Carrol sank to his knees. Thank God Frank was underground where the flies couldn't get him, instead of lying out there in South Park. A hot coal in his chest rose and tears burst from his eyes. He sobbed alone, watching the blurry road to Fairplay for riders. No one was going to catch Carrol Moncrief blubbering.

"God, I'm a wicked, selfish sinner," he moaned. "I want my brother back. I'd drag him out of the ground to have him back. I'd deprive him his reward, God. Forgive me."

His eyes ran dry, but he still felt the sick, hollow heat in his chest. He tore his hat off and threw it to the ground. Shifting his weight, he rolled to the ground and straightened his legs. He lay on his side, watching the road to Fairplay over the mound of Frank's grave.

"He was a better man than me."

How could this have happened? Frank was careful, professional. The convict who did this must have been some kind of cowardly sneak. Oh, when he found out . . . When he caught up to the bastard . . .

"Vengeance is mine, sayeth the Lord," he muttered. He had to get on top of that kind of thinking, or he would sin for sure. What would Frank do? Bring him in alive. Let the courts have him. Let God judge him. Oh, the Lord knew how to test a man.

A glint down the road caught his eye, and he pulled himself up quickly and began dusting himself off. By the time the buckboard came into view, he felt as presentable as his hard trip from Denver would allow.

A large cream-colored horse and a small black mule pulled the wagon. The sideboards bore the faded remnants of a painted sign that said SOUTH PARK SALT WORKS. Carrol knew the driver.

"Hello, Vernon," he said.

The driver flinched and peered through the tiny glass circles of his spectacles. The lenses must have caused the glint Carrol had seen down the road, for nothing else on the outfit shone. "Who's that?" he demanded.

"It's Carrol."

The scowl left Vernon's face, a look of sympathy taking its place. "Good Lord. Didn't expect you so soon." He set the brake on the wagon and felt his way down, reaching over the sideboards for a spade, a shovel, and a pickax as he lit.

"How's the salt of the earth business?" Carrol asked.

Vernon had come to South Park as a prospector, but settled for a claim with a salt spring on it and started evaporating brine in a cast-iron kettle. His salt was used in gold refining, and on dinner tables. For extra income, he contracted his grave-digging services to the county. "Dryin' up," he said. "Freighters startin' to haul salt in cheaper than I can make it."

"What do you figure to do about it?"

"Never mind," Vernon said, passing the graveyard gate. "I'm worried more for you than myself. Terrible thing that happened to Frank, but he's gone to his reward, and you don't need to worry about him."

"I know," Carrol said. "All I need to worry about is who did it."

"It was a fellow by the name of Dee Hassard. Said that was his name, anyway."

"Where was he from?"

Vernon squinted through his grimy lenses, found the place where he was supposed to dig. "Who knows?"

"What did he look like?"

"I didn't never see him close up, and my eyes is poorly, anyway. But there's a picture of him in the sheriff's office. A photograph."

"Photograph? There ain't no photographer in Fairplay, is there?"

"No, but you remember that government survey team that passed through the territory last summer?"

"Yeah."

"Remember that photographer among 'em?"

"Yeah. Fellow named Jackson."

Vernon threw his spade and shovel down and tested

the handle of his pickax. "Well, he passed through town with his photographic party the other day, headin' down to the San Juans this year. Happened to be here the day we brought Frank's body in. When he heard the name of Dee Hassard, he says, 'Wait just a darned minute! I made a picture of a fellow called Dee Hassard up at Denver 'while back.' Sure 'nough, he pulled the picture out, and it was the same little crook Frank was takin' to Cañon City when he got kilt."

Carrol nodded ominously. "What was Frank takin' him to prison for?"

"He swindled a bunch of gold dust from Sam Cornelius. Convinced Sam that he had discovered a diamond field in South Park, and Sam bought his claim." He spat on his hands, getting ready to dig.

"Diamonds?" Carrol said. "Sam fell for that?"

"This Dee Hassard was pretty slick. He almost got away with it, but they caught him in Denver and brought him back for trial." Vernon snickered and took his first swing at the ground. "He had already lost all Sam's money in a poker game."

The second thud of the steel point in the ground made Carrol shiver. "Whose hole you diggin' there?"

"Sam Cornelius's."

Carrol gawked at the grave-digger. "That flimflam artist got him, too?"

"No, a mountain lion kilt him over on the Tarryall."

"Mountain lion!" Carrol blurted. "What was Sam doin' over on the Tarryall, anyway?"

"Chousin' Dee Hassard. He got madder than get-out when he heard Hassard killed Frank and escaped. Took off trailin' Hassard and got et by that lion. Funny how the Lord works, ain't it?"

Carrol snorted. "Sometimes. Sometimes it ain't funny at all." He pressed his hat down on his head. "Take care, Vernon."

"You too, Carrol."

The preacher mounted his horse and rode at a trot into

Fairplay. He hitched his mount in front of the sheriff's office and walked in to find a deputy he did not know. "Howdy," he said. "You in charge here?"

The young man looked up from the load of paperwork he was shuffling through. "Yes, sir." He put his pencil down. "I'll bet you're the Reverend Carrol Moncrief."

Carrol smiled, touched by the recognition. "Wouldn't pay me to take that bet."

"You favor Frank a great deal."

"Only in appearance, I'm afraid. I've got some catchin' up to do in character."

"We all do, Reverend." The deputy stood and reached across the desk to shake Carrol's hand. "We didn't expect you this soon. We didn't know where to contact you. How did you find out?"

"A stranger in Denver told me. He had just come from here."

The deputy nodded and made a gesture inviting Carrol to sit. "Is there anything I can help you with?"

Carrol rattled the polished oak chair across the rough-sawn floor and sat down. "I was wonderin' about the headstone."

"The county's gonna pay for a big marble marker. We've been waitin' on you to approve the inscription." He reached into a desk drawer and removed a sheet of paper, which he handed to the reverend.

Carrol checked the name and dates, read aloud the part that said KILLED IN SERVICE TO PARK COUNTY. He nodded approvingly. "His favorite psalm was one hundred eighteen, verse six. I want you to put that on there, too."

"All right," the deputy said, reaching for a pencil and a piece of paper. "You'll have to refresh my memory, though. What does that verse say?"

"It says, 'With the Lord on my side, I do not fear.' But don't put the verse itself. Just put 'Psalms, One-eighteen: six.'" He stroked his fingertips across thin air, as if the polished marble stood between him and the deputy.

"That way some curious soul might look it up every now and then, and Frank will draw somebody new into the Good Book."

The deputy shrugged. "If that's what you want."

"That's what Frank would want. Now, I understand you've got a photograph of the man who murdered my brother."

The deputy opened another desk drawer and pulled out a file folder. "It's in here somewhere." He began thumbing through the large photographs in the file. "That photographer, Jackson, brought us a whole mess of pictures he made of Fairplay last year." He removed one print and flipped it across the desk to Carrol. "Here's one of the Snowy Cross," he said. "Figured you might want to see it, you bein' a preacher and all."

Carrol glanced at the picture once, then felt his eyes pull harder toward it the second time. He had thought Jackson some kind of fool for chasing after the legend last year, wasting taxpayers' money. But here was proof of Jackson's instincts and abilities.

And what proof! Where did such a mountain stand? Such a scene! It stirred the parson, accustomed though he was to mountain views. Those pure lines of white in that stark wilderness seemed to tell him something. Seemed to call his name!

"Here he is," the deputy growled. He handed the photograph of Hassard across the desk.

When Carrol pulled his eyes away from the Snowy Cross, the face of Dee Hassard all but shouted at him, and his brain raced to place the features. He knew this man. But . . . Where?

"The name he used here was Dee Hassard," the deputy was saying. "No tellin' what he's goin' by now . . ."

The moment rushed back at Carrol like a gunshot. He saw Dee Hassard outside the Denver saloon, kneeling, pretending his rebirth. A moment later, breaking the news of Frank's death. Fool! You stupid, trusting fool!

"Reverend?" the deputy said. "You all right?" The big

man had begun to tremble in front of him, his brown face darkening, one hand on the Snowy Cross, the other on Hassard.

Carrol looked up at the deputy. "I laid my hand upon his head. I blessed him. He didn't let on. He didn't show nothin'."

The deputy's mouth dropped open. "You've seen him? You've seen Hassard?"

Carrol twisted his features, fighting the hatred. "*He* told me about Frank." His fist clenched, crumpling the photograph, bending Dee Hassard's mouth into a cruel smile.

Thirteen

❧

$\mathbb{R}$amon stopped on the trail and let Sister Petra walk ahead. He wasn't tired; he just wanted to take in one more view of the San Luis Valley before hiking back into the village of Del Norte. This was a wonderful basin of green waving grass: too broad to cross in a day afoot, so long that it rolled over the horizons and disappeared to the south and north. White-topped peaks gathered it in, marked it, made it a world unto itself.

The little nun was well ahead of him now on the path that led back to Del Norte. He paused another moment to let his eyes sweep the valley. He would catch up with her easily before they reached the village.

It was as if Ramon had grown on this trek. His legs seemed to have lengthened, and now he could challenge Sister Petra's gait for hours a day. And he had grown in other ways. He had learned that the *penitentes* were really quite ordinary men. Before, he had thought of them as fiendish fanatics who nailed one another to crosses. But now he could greet the members of the brotherhood in each new village with neither fear nor prejudice. They were just men.

With Sister Petra, Ramon had sought the *penitente moradas* throughout the villages of northern New Mexico, and into southern Colorado. He had never dreamed so many towns existed in those hills and mountains. In Taos, he had simply stared in wonder at the sheer numbers of people, writhing in the streets like hornets on a nest.

"What are they all doing?" he had asked Petra.

"What do you mean?"

"Where are they all going? What are they doing?" It had aggravated him that he did not know, as he had understood all the comings and goings in Guajolote.

"They have their lives," Petra had answered.

"Yes, but . . . Like that man, there, with the wheelbarrow. Where is he going?"

"I don't know," she had snapped. "Am I supposed to know everyone's business in the world?"

They had continued north, out of the low sage and up to this high green valley of farms, grasslands, and remote Mexican villages.

It had been a kaleidoscope of places and people, but this was certainly the end of the journey, and Ramon was ready to turn homeward. They had come to the northernmost *morada* of the *penitentes* at the village of Del Norte, Colorado. They had followed the trail to the *Calvario* where each year one of the brothers would hang from the cross. Sister Petra had knelt to pray. She had received nothing from God. It was over. Everything northward was Anglo domain. There were no more *Calvarios* to climb. Guajolote was lost.

Perhaps God had taken a hand in it after all, Ramon thought as he broke into a trot to catch up with Sister Petra. Now he knew that there were other places to live. He could go back to Guajolote and comfort the people.

Yes, they would lose their homes, but the world was a big place. They would find new places to live.

When they reached the edge of the village, Brother Hilario rose from the ground where he had waited, leaning against the adobe wall. "Did you find what you were searching for?" he asked, a look of incredulity in his eyes.

"No," Petra said curtly. "I am going to pray now. I don't want to be disturbed."

She disappeared into the adobe Brother Hilario had provided for her stay, leaving Ramon with the local *penitente* leader.

Ramon put his hand on Brother Hilario's shoulder. "She is disappointed," he explained. "We have no place else to search, and still we haven't found the cross on the mountain. I think she is a little bit upset."

Hilario nodded. "Well, she has walked a long way for nothing. I didn't think she was going to find anything up there."

Ramon bristled a little at Hilario's tone. "Sister Petra believes in what she's doing. She doesn't pretend."

"I never thought she was a pretender, only a lunatic." The brother pulled his shoulder out from under Ramon's hand and turned back toward his home in the village.

Ramon glared at the back of his head as he walked slowly away. "I hope they hang you from the cross next time," he muttered under his breath.

They were strangers here. This was far from home. Nobody in Del Norte had even heard of Guajolote. It was time to turn back.

Ramon walked down the street and led his burro from the trough to the adobe where he and Petra would stay the night. Methodically, he began unpacking the *aparejo*. It had become a routine with him at each new camp or village. He had learned to travel well, and he was proud of it. Sister Petra would praise him to his father when he got back home.

Ramon and the green-eyed nun had arrived at an

unspoken truce after a few days of travel. He had stopped questioning her, and she had ceased to harangue him for laziness. There was respect between them now, and they traveled well together, though they knew little more about each other than when they had left Guajolote.

It made Ramon feel a little sad that Sister Petra would not find her cross on the mountain. This was important to her. It was real. He still found it a little difficult to comprehend. Nothing had ever been that crucial to him. He had no ambitions of achieving anything the way Petra felt she had to find that cross she thought God had told her about, in order to save a tiny village from being sold out from under its people.

"Good, you're unpacking the burro," she said suddenly, catching Ramon off guard. "Bring the beans and flour in, and we will make something to eat."

He lifted the sacks of food, turned, and noticed the smoke trailing from the adobe brick chimney. This was strange. Petra seemed in rather high spirits—almost renewed. She had built a fire. She had an appetite.

He brought the food into the adobe and put it on a table of rough pine boards. These were the rudest accommodations they had been given at any village. One window was covered with parchment, and another with some kind of animal skin—coyote, he guessed. But the fire in the beehive fireplace gave sufficient light, and they would only be staying here one night.

"Well," Ramon said, "what are we going to do now?" He would not mention going home. He had learned that it was best to let Petra think she was making all the decisions. He simply tried to steer her down the right path through suggestion.

"I don't know," she answered, "but I have prayed for direction, and I have faith that I will have my answer by morning."

Ramon nodded, carefully testing the ground of this conversation. "What do you think the answer might be?"

Petra smiled and took the bag of corn flour from him.

"You have been very patient, Ramon. Don't think I don't appreciate it, just because I haven't told you so."

"Yes, but . . ."

"I know, I haven't answered your question. I believe God will send us a sign in the morning, telling us where to search next. I don't know what the sign will be, but I have a feeling—just a feeling—that we are to continue going north."

Ramon dropped the bag of beans, spilling some across the pine table. "North!" he blurted. "That is Anglo country. That is fine for you, because you are Anglo. But what about me?"

Petra rolled her green eyes in the dim light of the adobe. "For your information, I am not Anglo. My grandparents came from France. *Anglo* means from England."

"You speak English, and that makes you Anglo. Besides, your skin is not brown, and neither are your eyes. You are *Americano*."

"Whether you know it or not, Ramon, you are American, too. You were born in New Mexico, a territory of the United States since 1848. I don't know what you're afraid of. You survived all those Americans in Taos, didn't you? You might as well get used to them. They're not going to go away. Traveling to the north will be good practice for you."

"But, I want to go home!" Ramon cried. "We are not going to find any cross on any mountain. Haven't we gone far enough?"

Petra's green eyes turned cold. "Go home if you want to. The brothers will help you find your way. But I am going to keep searching. God has told me what I must do."

Ramon flailed his arms and turned a circle in the dusty room. He didn't look forward to walking home alone. But what was worse? Following Sister Petra indefinitely northward? His face pinched in a scowl, and he lost his temper. "Oh, God has told you what to do! Just like my father's burro was talking to me just now outside!" he blurted.

Petra gasped and stared openmouthed at the boy. Then her face hardened like a chiseled statue and she pointed stiffly to a stool beside the table. "Sit down!" she ordered.

Ramon cowered under the little woman's glare and sank obediently down on the stool.

"I'm going to tell you something, and I don't care whether you believe me or not." She bent at the waist, the better to glare down at him. "All my life I have faced doubters, including my own friends and family, but I know what my calling is, Ramon, and your sharp tongue does not shake my faith. Now listen, and I will tell you why I have given my life to God."

The boy swallowed and looked at the fire to escape the sister's harsh glare.

"I was only twelve years old when I first heard the voice of God," she said. "Only, I did not just hear it. I felt it, absorbed it like a tree that is struck by lightning. My name then was Julie. I was fetching a bucket of water for my mother, and I was thinking about things a girl might think of. Like dresses, and friends, and school. Then the voice of God came at me from everywhere at once, swift and hot as a ray of sun, and it knocked me to the ground, and I spilled all of the water. And the voice had said to me: 'Serve them.' "

Ramon shifted his eyes suspiciously. "Serve who?"

"Be quiet. I am not finished." She braced her fists on her hips and looked down her nose at him. "After I heard those words, I forgot about friends, and new dresses, and school lessons, and I thought only about what God had said to me. I told my mother, and she did not believe me. She told me I had taken a heatstroke. It took me two years to convince her that I had heard the voice of God. And every day of those two long years, the children around me mocked and made fun of me, for I told everyone. I wasn't ashamed or embarrassed. Not like you, Ramon, when your friends call you padre. It was a great glory to me, and I knew I had to find out whom it was that God wanted me to serve.

"There was a convent, the Sisters of Loretto, at Nerinx, Kentucky. My mother took me there, and I gave my life to God. I became Sister Petra.

"I was twenty-one the next time I heard the voice of God. I was working in the vegetable garden, and something struck me down. Not painfully, like a blow, but swiftly and powerfully, as if I had been near an explosion. But there was no sound other than the voice. And when I awoke, I was on the ground, and dirt was sticking to the sweat on my face, and I remembered what God had said to me: 'Seek the blood of Christ.' The *Sangre de Cristo*."

"The mountains?" Ramon said.

"Yes, but I had never heard of the Sangre de Cristo Mountains then. It was another year and a half before I figured it out. Bishop Lamy came from Santa Fe seeking more nuns to serve in New Mexico, to teach in the schools and nurse the sick. This wasn't new to the Loretto convent. Sisters had gone west with Bishop Lamy before. The bishop was telling us about New Mexico, and he mentioned the Sangre de Cristos. I asked him what the name meant, for I was enchanted with the Spanish language. And when he told me, I knew that I was to go with him.

"I spent a while in Santa Fe, then I volunteered to serve at Guajolote, because there was no priest there, no chapel, no school. You may not remember how poor my Spanish was when I arrived five years ago, but I learned, and I served, and I waited again to hear that voice of light and power. And now I have heard God speak to me again, and he has told me that the cross awaits me on the mountainside. So you see, I must continue to search. I believe that God wants to save the village of Guajolote. And that is why he has spoken to me these three times in my life. I must serve him."

Ramon looked at the dirt floor of the adobe hovel. "But why would God choose one village? Why Guajolote?"

"That is for God to know. The Bible says that we will hear, and not understand; that we will see, and not perceive. I only do what God tells me to do. I have no choice. It is my life. I have heard the voice of God. I don't blame other people for not believing what I say, but I am not a perfect little angel, Ramon, and I get tired of it. So if you think I am lying, you can just go on back to Guajolote. I must continue." She turned her glare on the fire now, releasing Ramon.

He glanced up at her, saw the fire reflecting in her sharp eyes. "It's a shame," he said.

"What is?"

The boy shrugged. "You're not really that bad looking. I think you are too old to get a man anymore, but you have a pretty face, and nice long hair. You're almost too skinny, but that is better than being too fat. It is a shame you have to be a nun."

Sister Petra blushed and pushed a strand of hair back from her cheek. "Maybe you are trying to be nice now, but you are wrong. It is not a shame, Ramon. It is an honor. It is a glory. It is a burden and a responsibility, but it is not a shame. It is like nurturing a child, but the child is all of humanity. It is a labor, but it is a labor of hope and love. It is a blessing to be called, not a curse."

She looked at the boy and found him staring back at her, his brow wrinkled in the firelight. How much of this could he understand? She smiled. "I'm sorry I snapped at you. Tomorrow, if you decide to go home, I will understand. But that will make my journey more difficult, because you have become a big help to me."

Ramon looked away, feeling ashamed now for some reason.

"Do something for me if you will," Petra said.

"What, Sister?"

"Tonight, pray for direction. God hears all voices. If you pray, you will know what to do."

Ramon made a furrow in the dusty floor with his toe. It was not so much to ask for. Petra's style was to influence by example, not by directive. If she was coming right out and asking him to say a prayer, she must want him badly to do it. It wouldn't hurt anything.

"All right," he said. "I will."

Fourteen

❧

Petra woke when she sensed the morning light struggling through the parchment and animal-skin window coverings. She hadn't slept past dawn the whole trip, and she felt more than a little indolent for letting it happen today.

As she put on her shoes, she thought about waking Ramon and having him pack their things on the burro. But she had nowhere to go just yet. Perhaps it was better to let the boy sleep a while this morning. Maybe she could borrow some eggs or cheese and make Ramon a big breakfast.

She closed the pine door quietly behind her as she stepped out into the gray light of early morning. The sun had not yet risen over the Sangre de Cristos, far across the valley. She stepped around the corner of the adobe to take in the view of the basin and her eyes pulled northward.

The first ray of sun suddenly streaked through a far-away mountain pass and fell on a patch of whiteness above the village. It seemed to flare, like the burning bush on the mountainside. A body of motion took form around it, and Petra made out a rider on a white mule leading a party of men toward the village.

Something made her shiver, and she took a step toward the travelers. She counted them as they came nearer. There were seven men, each riding a horse or mule. A pack train of four mules walked among them. A couple of the beasts carried large black boxes such as Petra had never seen. She met the party beyond the outskirts of the town, and the riders pulled up their mounts to converse.

"Buenos dias," the bearded man on the white mule said. He looked wise for his years, gentlemanly. His accent was terrible.

"Buenos dias," Petra answered.

"Do you speak English?" the rider asked, his eyebrows rising hopefully.

"I ought to," Petra said. "I grew up in Kentucky."

The man smiled, swung down from the handsome white mule, and held his hand out to Petra. "Forgive me. I mistook you for one of the locals."

"I'm just a visitor here," Petra said, taking his hand.

"This is the village of Del Norte, isn't it?"

"Yes."

"I'm William Henry Jackson, chief photographer of the U.S. Geological Survey. This is the photographic party." He gestured toward his men.

Petra nodded at the riders, who tipped their hats. "I'm Sister Petra, of the Loretto convent in Santa Fe."

Jackson's eyes widened. "You're a nun?"

"Yes."

"What brings you here from Santa Fe?"

"I'm searching for a cross on a mountain."

Jackson smiled, his eyes twinkling. "You've seen my photograph."

"Pardon?" Petra said.

"I'm the one who made the photograph of the cross. It was on last year's expedition."

Petra felt her heart flutter. "You know of a cross on a mountain?" she asked.

The photographer wilted. "You haven't seen the photograph?"

"No."

"But you've heard of the mountain?"

"I've been told to seek the cross on the mountain. Could you tell me how to get to it?"

Jackson scratched the back of his head, tipping his hat down over his forehead. "Well, sure, but . . . What do you want to go there for? Some sort of pilgrimage?"

Petra's breath was coming in anxious gasps, but she was trying to appear calm. "I've been sent there."

"By whom?"

"God."

Jackson stifled a smirk when he read the conviction in the nun's eyes. "It's not an easy climb, Sister. It's in rough country, and you can only see the cross by climbing above the timberline."

"Who put it there?" Petra asked, trying to envision a cross on the high, barren slopes.

"*Put* it there?" Jackson shifted his eyes to his men around him.

"Yes. How did they get it so high up on the mountain?"

The photographer folded his arms across his chest and cocked one hip, as if posing for one of his own cameras. "Sister, what do you know about this cross?"

"Only what God has told me: that it awaits me on the mountainside." Her patience was teetering, but she paced herself.

"The cross I'm talking about was put there by God, Sister. It stands a good thousand feet tall. It's made of snow packed into crevices in the mountainside. I wish I had a print of my photograph to show you, but I gave the last one away in Fairplay."

Petra had raised her palms to her cheeks and was

staring with her mouth open. This was better than the time Bishop Lamy told her the meaning of *Sangre de Cristo*. She said nothing for a moment, wanting to taste the glory. Her heart was thumping in her chest, causing her to tremble. "How do I get there?" she finally asked.

Jackson pointed over his shoulder. "Well, you go north from here, up the San Luis, and over Poncha Pass. Drop into the Arkansas Valley and go upstream to Tennessee Pass. Now, there's an old Indian trail leading from Tennessee Pass to the base of Notch Mountain. Climb to the Notch Mountain Divide just south of the summit. You go above the timberline, and when you get to the top of the divide, you see the cross. That is, if it's not too cloudy up there."

Petra smiled, her eyes glistening. "How far is it from here?"

"If you came from Sante Fe, I'd say you're about halfway there. But it won't be easy, Sister. You'd better think twice about it. No white woman has ever been there. No woman at all, as far as I know. We had a devil of a time climbing there last year. Two helpers and I had to carry forty-pound packs to get the photographic equipment to the divide. It was too rough for the mules."

Petra waved his warnings away with a brush of her hand. "If you can make it with forty pounds on your back, I can surely succeed. I go with the strength of God. Now"—she clasped her hands before her and smiled at the messenger—"tell me the way again. Tell me what the cross looks like."

Ramon stepped from the dusty earthen house and rubbed his eyes. What was the nun up to this morning? Why hadn't she wakened him? He squinted as he searched the winding dirt streets, the cottonwoods along the river. His eyes swept across the San Luis Valley, past the glare of the rising sun, and northward, where they locked in on a group of men and beasts.

There she was! Who were those men she was with?

She was listening intently to one of them, her hands folded before her as if in prayer.

The man in front of her wore a beard, neatly trimmed, and gestured with his hands a great deal. He was describing something big—as big as a mountainside. His palms swept the morning air like the brushes of a reckless painter. Now he made fists, flung them open like bursting shells. Facing the nun, he put his feet together and leaned as far back as he could without falling. His arms rose at his side, straight and stiff as timbers. They leveled out, made a perfect cross of his body, then kept lifting, slowly, until his palms had risen just above his shoulders.

Sister Petra bounced on her toes like a little girl, lunged at the man, and hugged him under his uplifted arms.

Fifteen

꧁꧂

The drunker he stayed, the meaner he felt, and Charlie Holt liked the way the anger seethed. He knew that if he sobered up he might lose his resolve, quit the search for his runaway wife, go back to Kansas to be laughed at.

But if he stayed primed, he would have purpose. Maybe he would find her with another man. What would he do then? He had a notion. Maybe he would do some killing and turn outlaw. The thought appealed to him here in the saloon across from the shoe store. He saw it in hazy glimpses, like chapters of a dime novel he might have read once. There were gunshots, dead bodies, lawmen coming after him. Women who courted danger would open their doors. Men would stare in fear at his poster. Yes, Charlie Holt would have his own poster.

It had been easy to trail May this far. She was the kind of woman who caused the gazes of men to linger over her as she walked away. She had been remembered by the stage driver who gave her a ride into town in the middle of the night, the ticket agent who sold her the fare to Denver, the conductor who saw her enter the wagon yard near the depot.

Charlie had arrived in Denver yesterday, found the wagon yard she had stayed in a couple of nights. The man seemed nervous talking about her but said she had worked at a shoe shop a few blocks away the last he heard.

Charlie had been sober this morning when he found the shoe shop. Sober and weak of will; unsure of his ability to handle an unpredictable woman. He had sat in the saloon across the street for three hours now, watching the shoe store through the grimy glass. He was ready. Whiskey had stoked a fire in his belly. To hell with that farm. This could turn out to be the best thing that ever happened to him.

He remembered something his father had told him: "The true mark of a man lies in his ability to profit from his misfortunes." That was before his father died and his mother married that mean bastard with the hog farm.

He got up suddenly, pushing the chair out hard behind him. He slipped the half-full pint bottle into his breast pocket, slapped his dirty farmer's hat on, and strode for the door. The fire in his belly roared like a furnace. It was time for Charlie Holt to make some profit from the misfortune brought upon him by marriage to the faithless May Tremaine.

Stepping long across the street, Holt came to the door of the shoe shop and burst in, causing a cowbell on the transom to clang.

The cobbler glanced up as a customer counted coins and dropped them into his waiting palm. "Thanks," the cobbler said, casting the coins into a cigar box, which he closed and placed under his sales counter. "What can I do for you?" he asked, turning to Holt.

Charlie waited until the customer had left, then stepped

up to the counter. "I'm lookin' for May Holt—or May Tremaine—whatever she's callin' herself."

The cobbler's smile dropped. "She don't work here no more."

"Where'd she go?" Hold demanded.

"Now, look here," the cobbler said. "Who are you to bust into my shop and start askin' questions?"

"Name's Charlie Holt. I'm her husband."

The cobbler's eyes flashed once, then shifted nervously. "She never said she had no husband. I never heard nothin' 'bout no husband."

Holt sighed impatiently. Talking of May made all the men whose paths she had crossed turn nervous. He had his ideas as to why. "Just tell me where she went."

"Didn't show up for work one day. Hell if I know why. Next day I seen her with them pilgrims when they come into town to sell their wagons."

"Pilgrims?"

"Yeah, a bunch of fanatics called the Church of the Weeping Virgin. They put a pack string together and headed west toward Georgetown. Goin' over to the West Slope, I heard."

Holt sneered, but felt empowered by the news. He touched his brim and started to turn away.

"You want her things?" the cobbler asked.

"What things?"

"She left a shawl and a hairbrush and some other things."

Holt grabbed his lapels and glared. "She *stayed* here?"

The cobbler swallowed, sweat beading his brow. "Well, why not? Had to stay somewhere. I'll go get her things."

When the shoe man stepped into the back room, Charlie Holt felt an impulse sweep him up and knew he had to act on it or lose it forever. He reached over the counter and felt for the cigar box. Finding it, he lifted it into view, placing it on the counter. He flipped the lid quietly, his heart thrilling. He took the paper money first, wadding it in his pants pocket. Then he plucked a few gold coins, wincing at a metallic chink they made in his palm. He heard footsteps, closed the box, slipped it back under the counter.

"Don't know why she didn't come back for it," the cobbler said as he returned. He saw the man straighten and noticed the wild look in his eyes, mistaking it for anger.

Charlie closed his hand around the gold and crossed his arms, shoving both fists under his armpits. "Oh, hell, just keep that shit," he said. "Like you say, if she didn't come back for it, that's her own damn fault."

The cobbler felt awkward holding the handful of women's articles. He shoved them into his left hand and held his right over the counter. "Well, good luck findin' her," he said.

Charlie Holt felt several gold pieces in his right fist. He curled his lip and hissed at the cobbler with disdain. "Hell with her. I'm goin' back to Kansas." Turning toward the door, he pushed the fist into his pocket. It would be a good idea to get out of town about now.

Sixteen

Dee Hassard slung his blanket into the pine branches and tripped across a body in the dark. "Wake up!" he shouted.

A dream snapped in Clarence Philbrick's mind, and he sat up without thinking, his hand falling on the breech of his Remington.

"She came back!" Hassard was shouting. He stumbled shoulder-first into a bank of orange embers, rolling quickly away, regaining his feet. "Praise God, she spoke to me again!"

Elder Hopewell stirred with the pilgrims, annoyed at the disturbance of his much-needed rest. Yesterday they had crossed the Great Divide in a freezing rain by a mountain pass that stood above the timberline. His first look at the West Slope had been a frightening one, for he could see only bare rock below him in the storm. They had since descended into a deep valley of verdant grandeur, waterfalls plunging from rocky places in ribbons of froth. Hassard had pushed the party hard—too hard, Hopewell thought.

They had built a log ferry to cross the swollen Blue River, not even pausing to rest on the west bank. They had marched right through the new mining town of Frisco—the last settlement they would see. They had passed beaver ponds where the elder had hoped they might linger. Hassard had driven them relentlessly through a winding and sheltered valley that looked to Hopewell like a good place to settle. But the new prophet of the Church of the Weeping Virgin seemed to think of nothing but his pilgrimage to the Mount of the Snowy Cross.

The trek had been exhausting. And now this—to be woken from a sound sleep in the chilly night. Hopewell gathered his gangling legs under him and willed his eyes to focus in the dim moonlight, catching sight of the hysterical Deacon Dee stumbling across the congregation.

"I know what to do now," Hassard cried. "She told me!"

"Whoa, Deacon, whoa," Hopewell said, as if calming a skittish horse. He reached a long thin arm far across the camp as Hassard stumbled near him and grabbed the man firmly by the collar. "You're unsettlin' the people like that."

"Hopewell!" Hassard said, seemingly startled to find the elder there. "The Virgin came back! Where's the money?"

Clarence felt his coat for coins. Yes, it was still laden with gold, pressing heavily down on him as he got to his feet.

"Now get ahold of yourself," Hopewell said. "You're not making sense."

"It makes perfect sense," Hassard said, gripping the elder's arm. "It's just like Paster Wyckoff wrote in the *The Wisdom of Ages*! The faithful have to renounce everything that pretends to take power from God. That includes government, all those other false religions, and—money!"

"We have renounced all that," Hopewell said. "That's why we came out here, away from government power. Away from those other denominations. And we've given our money to the church."

Clarence stepped around the dazed pilgrims and stopped with the rifle stock on his hip. He looked back for May, remembering where she had bedded down on the spruce boughs he had cut for her. He saw her rising in the moonlight, as fine a sight as he had ever seen.

"And now it's time for the church to renounce that money!" Hassard yelled, raising his arms and laughing. "We're finally to be free of that 'evil mammon'—that's what Pastor Wyckoff called it. The Virgin came to me again tonight, Hopewell. Just now. And she told me why we're to make our pilgrimage to the Mount of the Snowy Cross. We're to sacrifice that money to God, there on the mountain. We're to give it up and trust in his will to get us by!"

"Wait a minute," Clarence said, stepping forward. "When you had these people sell all their wagons and things, you told them the money would be used to file on homesteads or buy government land."

"That was before the revelation!" Hassard hissed, waving his hand at the Vermonter. "Now I know better. What do you need money for? The wilderness will provide us everything. Now, where's the money, Elder Hopewell?"

"Hold on," Clarence said. "I see where you're entitled to a certain amount of authority as guide of this party, but that money belongs to these people. It's up to them to decide what to do with it."

"But it's not up to them," Hassard said. "It's not up to me, and it's not up to you. It's up to God, and God has sent his angel, the Virgin Mother of his only son, to tell Pastor Wyckoff, and now me, what the faithful are to do to save mankind!"

"But legally—" Clarence began.

"Legally?" Hassard stomped toward the Vermonter. "Brother Clarence, you haven't embraced what this church is all about. There is no law but God's law!" He seethed with a rage almost real in its vehemence.

Clarence remained unmoved. "If it were your money, you could do whatever you wanted with it. But . . ."

"Look," Hassard said, tromping off toward his saddle on the ground. "I understand your reservations. You haven't seen the Virgin weeping in your dreams." He fumbled excitedly with the flap of his saddlebags. "But maybe this will convince you."

Clarence scarcely saw the articles Hassard lifted from the saddlebags in the moonlight, but he could tell by the way the man handled them that they carried considerable weight for their size.

"I've got almost two thousand dollars' worth of gold dust here from my mine in Tarryall," Hassard said, carrying the two leather pouches to Elder Hopewell. "I didn't mention it before, because I was greedy. Thought you might want some for your church. But now I'm willing to give it all up!" He placed the two bags of dust in Elder Hopewell's hands.

"What do you want me to do with it?" Hopewell said.

"Add it to the church coffers." He took the roll of bills from his coat pocket and handed it to Hopewell. "Put this with it. And when the time comes, I hope you'll see fit to dedicating it to the Lord."

"Just what do you mean by 'dedicating' it?" Clarence asked.

"I am to find this mountain—the Mount of the Snowy Cross. I am to lead the faithful there. And we are to leave all our evil mammon at the place where we first catch sight of the cross. Those are my instructions from the Weeping Virgin. That is dedication, Brother Clarence. That is the dedication of the faithful!"

"That's throwin' money away on a mountaintop if you ask me."

A look of suspicion swept Hassard's face. "Maybe you'd like to have your share of the money back," he said. "Is that it, Brother Clarence?"

"No, that's not it, because I never put any money in there. I'm just against throwing money away when it might be put to some kind of good use."

Hassard put his hands on his hips. "Have you read *The Wisdom of Ages*?"

"Not all of it," Clarence admitted.

"How much have you read?"

"I only got through the first chapter."

"Brother Clarence, how do expect to become a member of this church if you don't read Pastor Wyckoff's book?"

"I never said I intended to become a member of this church—no offense to any of these folks. You just hired me on as a hunter for this trip."

"So you're here to make money, not to dedicate it. You seem to be struggling with inner greed, Brother Clarence."

"No," May said, the heads turning to look at her. "Clarence was real generous to me. He bought me supper in Denver when I was hungry and didn't have a place to stay."

In the sparse light, Hassard saw the eyes of the pilgrims shift from May to Clarence and knew he needed to add nothing to their suspicions. "I don't doubt he did. But he's said he doesn't intend to join the congregation of the Church of the Weeping Virgin, he's offered no money to the church coffers, he's failed to read past the first chapter of *The Wisdom of Ages*, and yet he thinks he has the authority to tell these people what to do with their money?"

"You're the one who's trying to tell them what to do with the church money. I'm saying it's up to them, not you."

Hassard took a few steps toward Clarence. "I'll tell you one thing I have the authority for. That's gettin' these good people safe to their promised land. To do that, I have to keep them fed, and I haven't seen you bringin' in any meat."

Clarence shifted the rifle in his hand. "Game's been scarce. Prospectors must have spooked everything out."

The deacon snorted. "You've got tomorrow to bring some meat in, or you're fired. Now, I'm goin' into the woods to pray. I'll say a special one for you, Brother Clarence. You need it." He walked through the throng, which parted to let him pass into the trees.

When he had skulked far enough into the timber, he stopped to urinate on a tree trunk, then grinned as he buttoned his trousers back. That Clarence from Vermont really thought he was something. He almost hoped that smart-mouthed kid did kill some meat tomorrow. Pulling this thing off would be a lot easier without him around, but it would definitely be more interesting with him.

He found a log on the ground and knelt beside it, lying across the top of it. He would sleep there, and someone would come to wake him before dawn and find him as if he had fallen asleep in prayer.

Oh, young Clarence was full of himself. But Dee Hassard had made fools of brighter men than him. If he couldn't get rid of the damn nuisance, he would just have to put a ring in the Vermonter's nose and break him to lead. And if that didn't work, there was always the rust-pitted Smith & Wesson or the fine blue Colt taken from the corpse of Frank Moncrief.

Seventeen

❦

Clarence sat against the trunk of a ponderosa pine, watching a small meadow take shape in front of him. His Remington rifle lay across his thighs, his right thumb on the hammer, left palm cupped around the forestock. Dawn was making the strange terrain known to him. He did not expect game.

This was lunacy. He should be in New Mexico by now, surveying his new domain, instead of lounging indolently in this strange forest. The Ojo de los Brazos waited to embrace him. Did the arms of May Tremaine?

The weight of fifty-six hundred pressed against his lungs, pulled at his shoulders. He felt like a fool right now. He was wasting his time. What if some other investor was snapping up the Ojo de los Brazos at this very moment? When his father found out, he would never hear the end of it. He wished at this moment that he had come west without the damned money. Look how far he had gotten on his wits. The money was only tormenting him, hurrying him through places were he might otherwise linger.

"Get the game, or go," he muttered to himself. This wilderness would decide for him. If he did not have meat on the ground by the time the sun bathed this meadow, he would leave the Church of the Weeping Virgin to fend for itself, and he'd turn south toward his destiny. He would not even rejoin the party. May would be with them. He would see her graceful limbs, meet her eyes, and lose his resolve.

I will have forgotten her by the time I reach Santa Fe. Good-bye, May Tremaine. Good luck. What will become of you while I build my kingdom down in New Mexico?

A sound swelled up under him, as if a heart had begun to beat in the bosom of the earth. His eyes searched as the Remington rose. The heartbeat thumped under him again, and he saw the buck deer bounding on four stiff legs at once. He pulled the hammer back, and the hooves came down again: the third heartbeat.

He shifted into shooting position as the buck landed broadside and froze. The irons found the shoulder. Black powder stained the air. The buck flinched and fell, quivering now on the ground.

The rhythm of the earth's heartbeat continued, coming now from the Vermonter's own chest. His ears rang, but he heard the echo of his shot glancing off some distant rim. The curve of an antler—bulbous and velvet-covered this time of year—stood above the grass no more than fifty paces from where he sat.

He got up and strode slowly toward the dead deer. From whence that buck had come, he could not say. It seemed to have sprung from the soil, surprising him. He had seen this happen with deer before, seen them materialize where moments before nothing had stirred. But this was fresh magic.

He approached the carcass and stood over it. A big deer compared to the whitetails he had hunted back in

Vermont. What had made him start bounding like that—drumming the earth with all fours like creation's own heartbeat? He had read in the sporting magazines that this was the way with blacktailed deer, hopping on four legs at once, but he had never dreamed it would shake the ground so.

He knelt, felt his grip take in the velvet antler, dreamed of riding into camp in glory. His doubts evaporated, and as he reached anxiously for his gutting knife, he knew he was in the right place, the right time. He was sick and tired of trying to live up to his father's expectations. This was where Clarence Philbrick belonged, whether there was any money in it or not.

Dee Hassard had turned the pilgrims onto a trail recently widened by the axes of prospectors . . . a trail used for centuries by dark-skinned huntsmen . . . a trail as old as the migrating herds who had trodden it bare long before any human shadow fell upon its ground. It led the faithful along the flanks of the Sawatch Range, toward Notch Mountain, where the view of the Snowy Cross supposedly awaited them.

May walked near the rear of the party this morning, glancing often over her shoulder. Her feet had healed and toughened nicely, thanks to the moccasins Mary Whitepath had given her. She might have paced the sojourners at the head of the pilgrimage, as she usually did, but something caused her to drop back today.

Strange how the pilgrims daily took their regular places in the processional, May thought. Some kept to the head of the line, some lagged, others habitually gravitated toward the middle. Back here, May was getting acquainted with a whole new set of believers. Faces she had seen around camp took on names, loosed voices.

"Are you plannin' to go all the way up to see the cross?" one said.

May looked into the tired but hopeful eyes of a young mother walking beside her. She couldn't place the accent.

Scottish or Irish, she guessed. Maybe Welsh. She wished she knew more about the world. "I don't know what I'm plannin'," she admitted.

The immigrant woman carried a baby in one arm, had a misshapen bag looped across one shoulder. Her other hand led a child tired of trotting, begging to be carried. "I'll follow Deacon Hassard there if I'm able," she said.

May glanced at the trail behind her. "Let me carry that baby for you," she said. "I don't have a load to pack."

"Thank you," the mother said. She handed the baby to May, swinging the heavier child up into her arms. "Are you ready to join yet?"

"I don't know that either. What all do I have to do?"

"You have to go through the initiation."

May drew her lips together. She was hearing more about this initiation all the time, the references always vague. "How come I can't just join?"

"Oh, there's things you can only learn in the three days. It's a secret. I can't tell you. But you'll be exhausted by the time it's done, I'll warrant that!" The little woman laughed at May, her eyes sparkling.

They strode on, May listening apprehensively to the immigrant woman make sketchy hints about the nature of the initiation. She would get no sleep, she would be starved, and she would be broken down to tears before it was all over.

"Why would anybody want to do that?" she asked, and the woman only laughed at her. She suddenly felt a thousand miles from civilization, caught up in something she didn't want or understand. Clarence was the only hope she had, and Dee Hassard had given Clarence the ultimatum.

As they came around a giant fir tree at a crook in the trail, May looked over her shoulder, and when she turned back to the way ahead, she found Dee Hassard in her path. She gasped, instinctively shielding the infant in her arms from the red-haired prophet.

"He ain't comin' back, Sister May," Hassard said.

She blushed. "Who do you mean?"

"You know. The kid from back east." He looked disapprovingly at the baby in May's arms, noticed the mother standing nearby as the rest of the party trudged on around them. "Brother," he said to a poorly clothed young man with several teeth missing, "carry this baby for this good mother. I want to talk with Sister May."

Reluctantly, May gave up the child as the mother drifted on up the trail with the rest of the party.

"I don't expect to see Brother Clarence ever again. He packed all his things with him and rode his own horse out this morning."

The tail end of the pilgrimage was coming around the bend in the trail now, shortly to leave May alone with the prophet.

"Did you see that in one of your visions?" she said, unable to mask her sarcasm.

Hassard smiled. This girl had seen and done more than she let on. "You don't believe in the Mount of the Snowy Cross?"

The last pilgrim, an old woman, limped around the crook in the trail, casting a parting glance at the pair—a fearful glance, it seemed to May—almost a warning.

"I don't know," May said, feeling vulnerable. She began walking again, but Hassard grabbed her by the arm.

"Wait," he said. "I want to talk to you about something."

She pulled timidly away, but he refused to release her. "Turn me loose," she said.

"Just a minute." He smiled, tightened his grip. "I won't hurt you, Sister May. I just want to talk."

She glanced down the back trail. No one was coming for her. Hassard was right. Clarence would never return. She was alone here with this stranger, deep in the forested mountains. The familiar fear surged all around her, the helplessness her aunt's husband had first introduced her to years ago.

"What do you want?" she said, her voice shaking.

"I want you to help me lead this rabble," he replied, testing her like strange snow-drifted ground. "People think more of a man when he has a beautiful woman by his side." He smiled, a thin expression of his power over her.

"They think enough of you already. You and your revelations. You don't need my help."

Hassard turned her toward him, his hand still firmly grasping her arm. "I know what I need, Sister May. Now, you think about it. This church will be the richest thing in the mountains before it's all over."

"I thought you were going to make them give all their money away."

"I mean land rich. God's green earth possesses more value than man-made coin. These people need a female model they can look up to. I think you fit the mold, May. You'll have everything."

"I don't know what you mean," she said.

"You know exactly what I mean. Ol' Deacon Dee has been around, Sister May. Enough to recognize that you have, too." He put another hand on her, crept his palms slowly up her arms, pulling her slightly closer to him.

May quivered, felt her disgust of the man being squeezed between them. Why did men like him always treat her this way? Damn him to think he could do this to her, lay his hands upon her, hold her here against his will! "All right, I'll think about it," she said. "Just let me catch up with the others."

"I will, May." He showed her how strong he was, pulling her toward him until her palms pressed flat against his chest. "But you've got to make up your mind soon. I go out in the woods to say my prayers every night. If you decide you want the easiest life in these mountains, you come on out and join me there. If you don't, this wilderness could be a little hard on you."

As his leer descended on her, she drew her face back, then turned her head sharply away. She thought she would burst with shame and hopelessness until she saw the figure rise from a dip in the trail downhill. "Clarence!"

Hassard glanced and felt his grip melt from her arms as she pulled away. He saw the antlers jostling, the broad body of the deer slung over the saddle. The hunter was leading his horse, grinning at May as she trotted to meet him. The Vermonter swept his hat from his head, its brim rolled in his hand.

"Damn!" Hassard muttered. He backed away as May reached the hunter. He stepped around the big fir in the crook of the trail. How had that kid managed to kill that deer? Sister May wouldn't be coming to join him in the woods tonight—he knew that. They meant trouble now—both of them.

Every scam he had ever had fail had failed because of a woman. Even that diamond field fiasco. He would never have gotten caught in Denver if he hadn't stopped at that whorehouse to gamble and fornicate.

Now Sister May had taken a peek under his prophet costume. How much would she tell young Philbrick? Damn those inviting eyes!

Eighteen

❧

Carrol Moncrief stalked slowly down the street, his eyes searching for bits of shattered glass. This was the place to begin trailing Dee Hassard. Not so much as a reader of sign, but as a calculator of men.

The hooves of a hundred horses had broken this ground since Hassard knelt upon it. A thousand drunken miners, cowboys, and vagabonds had obliterated the tracks the swindler had made leaving this street. Still, this was the place to begin, where they had stood together, the swindler hoaxing the preacher, the preacher deceiving himself.

A shard of glass twinkled in the noonday glare, and Moncrief squatted to pinch it between two toughened digits. Once he found the first, others seemed to sprout all around him—like gems in Dee Hassard's ludicrous field of diamonds. This was where the whiskey bottle had rained down on them in pieces. Where Carrol had met his brother's murderer.

The question was why. Why had Hassard made himself known to Carrol that night? He had shown his face, given the preacher a firsthand sighting, a lead. Was Hassard simply so mean that he wanted to see the look on Carrol's face when he broke the news about Frank? Or was he clever?

Let's assume he's clever, Carrol thought. No, more than just clever. Sly. Treacherous to the point that he didn't mind getting on his knees in the sight of God and everybody else in order to draw a victim into a snare.

But which snare?

Hassard had wanted him to go back to Fairplay for some reason. Carrol rolled the jagged piece of glass between his fingers until a new facet glinted at him. Maybe he had been looking at this thing wrong. Maybe Hassard didn't want him in Fairplay so much as he just wanted him out of Denver.

Still, why?

Moncrief felt his fingers tightening with frustration until a sharp point cut through his thick skin. He flinched, flicked the shard of glass aside.

All right, let's start over, he thought. What does a confidence man want? He wants something you've got. Something valuable. He wants it so bad he's willing to work for it, and work hard. Most people don't realize that a swindler is not a lazy criminal. Deception is hard work. Hassard's motivation lay not with indolence, but in the taking—the actual theft by swindle. It gave him a perverse sense of mastery to so smoothly steal.

He strode slowly toward the board sidewalk, mulling it over, stopping only to let a buggy pass. What did he have that Hassard would want? Where would Hassard go to get it? He kicked the board sidewalk where he and Hassard had talked religion. What were the last words that had passed between them? He had asked Hassard to inform the Church of the Weeping Virgin that he would not be available to lead them over the mountains.

So what? It wasn't as if Hassard would actually do him that favor out of the goodness of his heart, for not even the hole where his heart should have been held any goodness.

What had ever happened to that bunch of fanatics, anyway? Whom had they hired to lead them over the mountains? Oh well, that wasn't his concern. He had to catch Hassard. But there were no leads. The man could be anywhere.

The coward had killed Frank in cold blood and all but boasted of it to Carrol's face.

He spat in the street and fought an urge to utter a cuss word that was whirring in his head like the wings of a locust. Investigating had been Frank's strength, never his own.

In his old days of lawlessness, Carrol Moncrief had shaken many a lawman and vigilante from his trail. It was so easily accomplished. Only Frank had succeeded in riding him down, jailing him, seeing him to the penitentiary.

He had hated Frank for it at the time. "You ain't no brother of mine," he had told him. Now Carrol knew that he would have been dead and in hell by this time if Frank hadn't taken him down that hard reality road.

How had Frank done it? In those days no one could ride harder than the outlaw Carrol Moncrief. And yet his own brother had managed to bring him in. How? Simple enough. He made it more than a job. He made it personal. He just kept coming. That was what Carrol would have to do to catch this Dee Hassard, or whatever his real name was. Never quit, never stop thinking like a confidence man. Just keep coming.

He smacked his lips and looked at the sign on the saloon front. Parting the double doors, he stepped in, his eyes meeting those of the bartender almost instantly.

"Remember me?" he said, his spurs singing loud against the board floor.

The bartender's quick glance lashed his shotgun under the bar, then returned to the preacher. "You've got sand in your craw to come back here after pullin' that hog leg on me."

"Dry sand," Carrol said, throwing a coin onto the bar.

"You think I'll pour you good whiskey?"

"One thing I've learned about bartenders," Carrol said, hooking his heel on the foot rails. "You're forgivin' souls. I guess you've got to be when your best customers are drunks." He smiled with genuine warmth.

The bartender smirked, reached for a bottle and glass. "You're the damnedest preacher I ever saw. I thought the Good Book was supposed to be against drink."

"Against drunkenness, not drink. Jesus himself changed water to wine. Man's got to know when to quit, that's all."

"I hope you don't aim to hang around here all day and go to preachin' again."

Carrol took a sip and shook his head. "Just came to clear the cobwebs. I'm lookin' for somebody."

"Who?" The bartender's eyes brightened, hoping he could help move the preacher on.

"A fellow named Dee Hassard. Little redheaded peckerwood was here last time I was."

"Not the one you Christianized out there in the street?"

Carrol set his glass on the bar. "You remember him?"

"I heard the shot, like everybody else. Looked out the window to see what was goin' on. Saw that redheaded feller on his knees. You must have put the fear of God into that soul, Parson."

"How's that?" Carrol was straightening, sensing a fresh turn in the trail.

"He up and joined that bunch of fanatics the next day. You know, the pilgrims goin' over the mountains. Came into town with some of 'em to swap their wagons for mules and burros. Hell, looked like they was joinin' him, instead of him joinin' them."

"What do you mean?"

"He was ramroddin' the whole outfit. Had 'em sellin' wagons, furniture, all sorts of things. Later on I seen 'em leadin' a pack string back up toward Cherry Creek. That redheaded feller was on the lead mule."

Carrol smiled and picked up his glass. "Friend," he said, pausing to throw the last of the whiskey down his throat, "I'm sorry I ever pulled my pistol on you." He faced the handful of men in the saloon, raising his hands as he turned. "Bless this saloon!" he cried, closing his eyes tight. "May God bring only health and prosperity to all who enter its portals!" He made his head tremble for emphasis. "May every jigger poured here cleanse the soul of he whose veins it courses! Amen!"

"You ain't gonna start preachin' to my customers again, are you?" the bartender asked as Carrol Moncrief strode long for the door.

"Nope."

"Where you goin'?"

Carrol stopped at the door, his eyes flaring as they shot back across the barroom. "Over the mountains, brother bartender. I think it's time I went on a pilgrimage."

Nineteen

◈

The town was called Buena Vista, but the view did not look so good to Ramon. He hadn't seen one brown face since he arrived, nor heard a single word of Spanish—not even from Sister Petra. She had been murmuring that gibberish called English to virtually anyone who would listen.

The surrounding mountains were spectacles such as Ramon had never seen, hence the name of the bustling mining town. But the name was the only thing Spanish about this place. The peaks were not like the ones that rose above Guajolote. These were American mountains. Not Spanish, or Mexican. They didn't even seem like Indian mountains, though Petra had told him they belonged to the Utes. This was strange country—white man's domain—and he did not belong.

The people here gawked at him as if they had never seen a Mexican. Perhaps it was not Ramon, himself, so

much as it was the trio—the boy, the nun, and the burro.
It appeared to Ramon that word of them had spread since
they arrived an hour ago, and now every soul in town
wanted to get a look at the strange little party that sought
the cross on the mountain.

They were on their way out of town now, which gave
him some relief. But they were heading ever farther
north, which only made him feel sick for the familiarities
of home. Everything had slipped hopelessly beyond
Ramon's control. There was no way he could abandon
Sister Petra now and make his own way back to Guajolote. He didn't speak the language of this place. There
were no friendly societies of *penitentes* to provide him
with direction and sustenance. He hated feeling this de-
pendent on the nun, but he clung to her like a child to its
mother.

Worst of all, the bitterness and homesickness he felt
was beginning to make him doubt her. They had actually
gotten along very well since Del Norte—working together, entertaining each other with conversation and stories. Still, he was beginning to have an evil thought.

It had first occurred to him when they crossed Poncha
Pass, leaving San Luis Valley and all its Mexican settlements behind. It struck him then that the Anglo photographer they had met in Del Norte had spoken only English.
Sister Petra had been the only one in the village able to
translate for him. What if she had lied about what the
photographer said? What if she had simply made up the
story of this white man photographing a cross on a mountain? How would anyone know the difference? Petra was
the only one who spoke the photographer's language.

This was the idea that burdened Ramon with guilt—the
notion that Sister Petra was a liar. It was a sin to think
such a thing of a nun, but he couldn't help it. She could
have been lying to him all along for all he knew. God
might never have spoken to her in the first place. Maybe
she was just plain crazy.

The road led them out of town and up the rocky valley

of the Arkansas River, a stream of white water, rushing like the Anglos back in Buena Vista who seemed ceaselessly to scramble for wealth or influence, or whatever it was that drove them so.

"What's wrong with you today?" Petra said to him as they mounted their familiar gait—an easy rhythm, efficient in its regularity.

"I'm keeping up," Ramon said defensively.

"Not that," she replied. "You haven't spoken in hours."

He turned his head from her and sighed. He really didn't want to talk about it. "Did they say anything about the cross back there?"

"Oh, I'm sorry, I should have told you," she said. "Yes, everybody around here has heard of it, though I met no one who has actually seen it. They said the Indians first spoke about it, but they didn't really believe the Indians. Then, several years ago, an old prospector got lost— turned around up in the mountains—and he went above the timberline trying to find his way. As he came over a divide, he suddenly saw the cross. And then, he found his way all of a sudden, like magic!" She beamed her pretty green eyes at him.

Ramon looked away. "And where is this old prospector now?"

"Oh, he wandered away long ago. That is the way with prospectors, always searching for new diggings."

He rolled his eyes a little, almost hoping that she noticed. "And what about the photographer?"

"They didn't know of him, but that is because he never came through Buena Vista on his expeditions. One man I met had heard of the geological survey, though—the Hayden Survey, as he called it."

Ramon slapped his palms against his thighs, flailing the lead rope of the burro that had plodded so stupidly along with him on this ridiculous quest. "So we still have no guide to take us to this mountain, this cross, this vision of yours."

"It was never a vision," she said, her voice hardening.

"And we do have a guide, of sorts. We have the directions given to us by the photographer."

"Given to *you*," Ramon blurted. "I heard only *Ingles*."

"But I translated it for you," Petra said. She stopped in the road. "You believe me, of course."

Ramon took a few steps, then stopped. He did not turn to look back at her.

"Ramon? You *do* believe me?"

He wheeled, glared at her. "Of course! You are Sister Petra, the Divine. God talks to you, like me talking to this stupid burro to hurry up, or to get his foot off of the rope! You could not be a liar. You are too perfect."

She felt suddenly disappointed in him. He hadn't thrown a fit in many days, and she had come to think that he had grown beyond that. Now he was acting like a little boy again. She stalked off the road, toward a big rock near a slow bend of the river, in the shade of a cottonwood. "I am no more perfect than you are," she insisted as she passed him. "We will eat our lunch over here. Maybe we can catch some fish for tonight."

"Wouldn't that be *perfect*," he grumbled.

"Stop that!"

"I can't. I'm not a perfect angel like you. I have sins in my heart. Great big ones! Maybe one of them thinks you are a liar, but that could not be, because you are so perfect."

"Then why am I mad enough to pull your little nose off?" She clawed at the packsaddle, looking for the dried meat and fruits.

"You know what!" he said. "It would have been easier just to leave Guajolote and move to some other village than it is following you all this way on this stupid trip."

"I am not interested in what is easiest for you. I am interested in what God tells me I must do."

"Why? To save a little village nobody even cares about? Not even the church cares about it, because if they did, they would send us a priest instead of just a nun. Why would God want to save a little place like

Guajolote, anyway? It doesn't matter to anybody. What do you think you're going to find, if you ever see this cross? How is it going to help?"

"Neither you nor I know how God works. We must simply do his will."

"No, *you* must because you are so perfect. I am only here because my father made me go, and I was too stupid to disobey him."

"For the last time, Ramon, I am just as human as anybody else. Quit called me perfect, or I will prove to you that I am not!" She raised her hand threateningly.

Ramon was beyond fear of the little woman. Maybe she would slap the devil out of him, but he was willing to risk it in order to speak his mind. "What sin did you ever commit?" he said. "I bet you never even had a thought to do anything wrong."

"You want me to brag about my sins? That is preposterous! I don't have to prove my humanity to you by my sins!"

"Ah!" he shouted. "That's what I thought. You don't have any to brag about!"

She gathered her lips together in frustration and pounded a half loaf of rock-hard bread down on the boulder. "All right, Ramon! If you really must know, I will tell you one. Oh, you want to hear a *big* sin, don't you? Well, fine. I will tell you one. When I lived in Santa Fe . . . When I was at the Loretto convent there . . . Well, it was a very difficult time for me, and . . ."

"And what?" Ramon demanded.

"I had impure thoughts!"

His face writhed in wicked laughter. "Not *thoughts*!" he cried. "Now you are going to hell with the rest of us, Sister Petra!"

"It was not just the thoughts! I *acted* upon them!"

The mocking leer dropped from Ramon's face. "*Impure* thoughts?" he said quietly.

"Now you see that I am just as wicked as everybody else, don't you?" It was a little like bragging, she realized. It did suddenly put her on more even footing with Ramon, and that was what was needed.

"Wait a moment," he said, still uncertain as to whether or not he and Petra understood each other. "What exactly happened?"

She hesitated. The truth was she wanted to tell him. She had always wanted to tell somebody but had been too afraid. She had never even confessed it to a priest, which had driven her guilt even deeper. But she had come a long way with Ramon and gotten to know him well. Perhaps she owed him this. He was a good boy. They were friends now. Maybe this would help him to keep going somehow. She felt one thing for certain: Ramon might not agree with everything she dragged him through, but she could trust him.

"You have to promise never to tell anyone," she said. "Ever. If you do, I will commit another sin when I get my hands on your neck!"

"I won't tell," he said, sitting on the boulder to break a piece of bread.

She looked away from him. "You must understand that it was not an easy time for me," she began. "I had grown into a woman and was starting to regret that I had never done the things most girls do. I was beginning to doubt. The words God had spoken to me before seemed like a dream. I began to think maybe I had imagined them or something. Like my mother said: a heatstroke. I didn't know if I was supposed to be a nun all of my life. I was alone in Santa Fe, and I was confused."

"Yes, yes," Ramon said, urging her along with gestures. "Get to the impure thoughts."

She frowned at him. "I was teaching at the orphanage for girls, and there was a carpenter who came there to build a new staircase. He was an American from Kentucky, like me. His voice reminded me of home, and I liked talking to him. He was about my age—about twenty-five—and he was very good looking.

"Well, we became friends, and I started thinking about

him all the time, wondering what I had missed. So I
decided to find out. I knew it was wrong. I knew it went
against my vows. But that is the way with sin. It makes
you enjoy your betrayal of God. That is the true evil
of it."

"So . . ." Ramon said, trying to avoid the sermon and
get back to the story. "What did you do with the
American?"

"I told him the truth. That I wasn't sure I wanted to be
a nun anymore. He told me he would help me find out.
He rented a room. We met." She shrugged as if she had
said all she intended and picked up a piece of cured meat.

"But what did you do together?" Ramon demanded.

"Oh, come now. Your father raises chickens and goats,
does he not? You know about the birds and the bees."

"Ay!" The boy gasped with quiet astonishment, as if he
were talking now to some explorer returned from exotic
lands. "How did you know what to do?"

"I didn't. I was terrified. I felt clumsy and foolish. But
he knew."

Ramon chewed a piece of jerked beef for some time in
silence. "What happened after you met the American
there?"

"I was a little disappointed, once it was done. It wasn't
all I had expected. I felt guilty, too. Ashamed that I had
broken my vows in such a way. And yet, the pure thrill of
sinning was part of me now, and I didn't want to let that
thrill go."

"Did you meet him again?"

"Yes, I met him every now and then, when we could
arrange it. Our affair lasted about two months." Embarrassed, she put her fingertips against her forehead to
shield her eyes.

"What happened after two months? Did somebody find
out?"

"No one ever knew but he and I. He was a decent
young man, as some sinners are, Ramon. He was just led
astray. By me, I suppose. Anyway, after two months

went by, I realized something. I had been waiting for a feeling that would tell me I should quit the order to marry this man. I was waiting to fall in love with him, in other words, but it wasn't going to happen, and I knew it."

Ramon shook his head. "I bet you broke his poor heart."

Her eyes cut toward the river. "That was the greatest sin of all. And for that I felt so terribly shameful, Ramon. You will never know. It was a terrible thing to do to another person, to myself. And most of all, to God. I had made promises, Ramon, and had broken them in the most selfish way—right in the sight of God!

"I dictated my own penance, and I was more severe on myself than any priest or bishop would have been. Even the pope!"

"What did you do?" Ramon asked, thinking of the physical rigors the members of the brotherhood forced themselves to endure.

"I banished myself to Guajolote. Where there were no handsome young men who spoke in Southern drawls. Where there were no markets, or artists, or grand festivals. I banished myself to that dusty little village of yours and begged God that some good might come of my sins.

"And some good will come of it, Ramon. My faith is restored. God has forgiven me. And I have learned to love that remote little place. It is strange how the Good Lord works. It is almost as if he wanted me to sin." She shook her head. "It is more than I can understand."

"Maybe it's better that you committed that sin," Ramon said. "If you hadn't, you would always be wondering. I know I would."

"Ah, but that is the nature of faith, Ramon. You accept the road God gives you. You have faith that it is the right and only path for you. And you do not wonder anymore."

The boy dusted some bread crumbs from his shirt and remembered what she had said about fishing. There was a line and a hook in the pack, and various bugs around to use for bait.

"I'm going to try to catch a trout," he said. "You might as well take a siesta. It doesn't take two people to catch a trout."

He secured the line, caught a grasshopper. Before he went to the river's edge, he saw Petra spreading a blanket to lie on under the shade of the pine. "Sister," he said. "I am sorry I called you a liar."

She smiled, waved him away with her graceful little hand. "There will be none of that." Kneeling, she added, "Ramon, I have not had a friend like you in a long time. A very long time."

Twenty

꒜

Easy money spent fast. This Charlie Holt had learned by the time he got to Frisco. He was all but broke when he left the café, but his stomach was full of venison steak and fried potatoes, and he had just enough stolen cash remaining from the shoe store till to get mildly drunk, which was exactly what the outlaw in Charlie needed right now.

The valley lay cooling as he walked to the nearest saloon, the sun having plunged beyond the Sawatch Range. This wasn't like Kansas, he thought, where the blazing summer daylight scalded you hour upon hour in the fields. This was life such as Charlie had only dreamed of. This was the outlaw trail. Why he had ever lived another way was a mystery to him.

He was only three or four days behind the Church of the Weeping Virgin and closing ground fast. The pilgrims seemed to be moving at a pretty good clip for a party afoot, but Charlie had been riding hard, swapping for fresh horseflesh at every mining town. The roads up here were mere ledges carved out of mountainsides, but they tended to channel most travelers through the same passes, down the same valleys. The church had been easy to follow. With one more fresh mount, Charlie would be on them.

Lordy, but May was going to be surprised to see him. She was likely to piss herself. He would make her regret running away when he caught her.

The only problem was that Charlie was nearly broke. He didn't have enough money left from the "Denver Job," as he had come to think of it, to purchase a fresh mount plus the supplies he would need to push into the wilderness. Frisco was his last chance to get outfitted.

He stepped through the open door of the saloon and returned the suspicious gazes of the men who sat hunched over their drinks. It was a shotgun-style frame building—narrow where it fronted the street, running deep under a low ceiling. Two windows allowed a little grime-filtered daylight into the front of the saloon, but the back seemed dark as a bear cave, the bartender having not yet lit the coal-oil lamps.

A pair of townsmen broke their conversation to watch Charlie walk past their table at the window. They wore garters on their white sleeves. He strode the narrow path between the long rough-sawn bar and the two-seater tables against the wall. None had more than a single man sitting at it—dirty miners, most of them. Beyond the bar, calls and raises slowly circled a big table in a torpid poker game. Behind the big table, a back door led to a small dark space of some kind.

Charlie found a single high stool at the end of the bar and sat with his back to the poker game where he could watch the front door, drink, and plan his next job. He slapped a three-dollar Indian-head gold piece against the bar. "Give me a bottle of your slowest-sippin' whiskey. I've got time to kill."

"You come to the right place," the bartender said. "We've kilt more time here than Congress." He plucked the coin from the bar as he lay a glass in front of the stranger. "You must have come up from below with that government coin."

Charlie nodded, noticed where the bartender threw the three-dollar piece. "Kansas."

The bartender chortled as he poured the stranger's first drink for him. "Come to get rich off the diggin's?"

Charlie shrugged. "One way or the other."

As dusk came on, the saloon man lit the lanterns, and new customers sifted in off the rutted street. A comforting hum began to chase the tense afternoon silence from the room. Every now and then, Charlie noticed the bartender cutting notches into pieces of board that he kept stacked under the bar. He didn't know why and didn't really care.

After dark, he inquired about a privy, and the bartender pointed to the back door beyond the poker game. The door led to a small dark landing at the bottom of a flight of stairs. The stairs led to the saloon owner's room, he guessed. He turned the other way, went outside, and found the outhouse.

Returning to the saloon, Charlie found his stool taken, so he stood at the bar and watched men swap gold dust for drinks, the bartender measuring each purchase on a set of scales.

This saloon couldn't be old, Charlie Holt mused, for the paint had yet to peel anywhere in the whole town of Frisco. But the ceiling was already smoke stained, the walls whiskey spattered, the floor heel gritted. He wondered if he would be the first to rob the place.

He had already figured out how he would do it. The bartender-owner lived upstairs, he had learned, and usually closed his doors around dawn to catch some shuteye. Charlie would leave by the back door some time tonight, as if he were going to visit the outhouse again. But instead, he would go upstairs and wait for the tired barman. He would use his gun barrel on the bartender's head. He would have just enough time to raid the till, buy his supplies, and get back on the trail of his wretched run-away wife before somebody found the bartender bound and gagged.

"What?" the bartender said sharply, turning to a small tarnished mirror behind the bar. "Have I got lice on my head or somethin'?" He began searching his scalp for vermin.

Charlie poured another glass of whiskey, realizing he had been staring at the bald spot on the bartender's head—the spot he would split open with his pistol barrel. "Maybe just a nit," he said. Someday when the name of Charlie Holt was known all over these mountains, this bartender would entertain his customers by showing them the scar the outlaw scribed on his head.

"Block and tackle." The voice came like gravel slung from a prospecting pan.

Charlie glanced to his right, found an ancient miner there, dirt clinging to his shirt where it had stuck to sweaty places. The old man had dusted his clothes of everything that would shake loose, washed his hands and his white-bearded face. He smiled as his burled hand took a brimful glass from the bartender, and his face wrinkled like a map of the bad lands.

This fellow was a regular here, Charlie thought. The bartender didn't take any money or dust from him, just made a notch in a board with a pocketknife. The board had the name BILLINGS written on it in pencil.

"Block and tackle?" Charlie said as the prospector took his first drink.

The old man grinned. "Make you walk a block and tackle anything." He thrust his open palm toward the stranger. "Jules Billings."

"Charlie Holt," he said shaking the hand.

As the night wore on, they got vaguely acquainted, the bartender adding notches to Jules's wooden bar tab. By midnight, Charlie's bottle was half full and Billings was misty eyed.

"Prospectin' up here?" the old-timer asked.

Charlie scoffed. "Don't know the first damn thing about it."

"Tell you what"—Jules Billings was feeling the magnanimity of drink—"you can come to work for me till you learn the trade."

The outlaw Charlie Holt chuckled. "Learn prospectin' from a man who pays for his drinks with notches on a stick?"

Jules looked over both shoulders and leaned toward the stranger to speak low. "Boggs don't know it yet, but I'll settle my tab with him tomorrow. Ol' Jules Billings pays his debts."

"With what?"

"I finally hit a good one, Charlie," he said, as if they were old friends. "Filed the claim on it today. Sure, I've had some strikes play out on me before, but this one's wide as a gate. I worked it three days to make sure. Washed more than a hundred dollars' worth of dust a day with just a pan and a shovel."

"No shit?" Charlie said. "Gold dust?"

The prospector grinned and hoisted his right leg. He lifted his trouser leg over his boot top and made out as if scratching an itch on his calf. "What do you think of that? It's plumb full of gold dust."

Stuck into the top of the rawhide-laced boot, lashed tight against the prospector's leg, Charlie saw, was a small drawstring pouch bulging with its contents. He grinned out of one side of his mouth. "Boss," the outlaw said, "I'm with you."

"Let's go somewhere we can talk over terms," Jules said. "Hell, I might make you a partner if you'll carry your half."

Charlie grabbed his bottle by the neck. "Where do you want to go?"

"There's a quiet little whorehouse on the edge of

town," he said. "Hell, half the business deals in town get cinched there." He tossed his head at Boggs, pulled his hat down on his brow, and stepped back from the bar.

"Let's go out the back," Charlie suggested. "I need to visit that privy."

Jules Billings shrugged, gestured toward the back door, and fell in behind Charlie. This was more than the old man had hoped for. After so many false mother lodes, his reputation as a prospector was such that he could scarcely hire an employee, much less get one to throw in with him on shares. He knew when he came to town that he was going to have to find a greenhorn so new to these diggings that he had never heard of Jules Billings's dubious reputation.

This Charlie Holt is perfect, he thought, grinning as he peeked at the poker hands around the big table. The man has calluses on his hands—no stranger to hard work. He said he was broke, needing a stake. He'll settle for a quarter interest, sure. Hell, that'll make Charlie Holt richer than just about anybody in town. Except for me, that is.

He felt a blast of glory surge through him as the cold night air filled his lungs. He thought of his claim again—the best he had seen since California in forty-nine. This secret had been roiling in him for days, now stirred by the stout drink. He slammed the door behind him, leapt from the wooden steps, and pushed a wolf song up his throat.

"What the hell?" the outlaw said, startled, reaching for his pistol.

Jules laughed. "Tonight's my night to howl, Charlie." His head fell back and he took in the field of stars above, so bright through the thin air of the moonless mountain night.

"Shit," Charlie said. "I thought you'd gone loco." His heart was pounding like a monster's.

"Just feelin' close to God. Like the song says: 'I once was lost, but now am found.' "

"Which way is that outhouse?"

"Over yonder," Jules said, pointing.

"Lead the way, will you? I don't know this place."

"Come on, I'll get you downwind of it, then you'll find it easy enough." He laughed as he strode down the slope toward a little draw.

Charlie Holt's hand was still on his pistol grip, and now he eased the weapon quietly from the stiff leather holster. He had to step quick to come close behind the old prospector. The man began to whistle. Perfect. The poor idiot had no idea. Charlie's chest burned like a furnace as he reached for Jules Billings's hat brim, his pistol hand already swinging overhead like a windmill blade.

The cold air and the blue steel struck Jules's head together as he tried to turn, and he fell to his knees. The outlaw struck him again, grunting with the effort he put into the blow, feeling the body give under the impact, hearing the sick thud that gave him such twisted satisfaction. The old miner fell on his side, unconscious.

Charlie Holt put his pistol back in the holster, drew it again, pointed it at his victim, shook his head, put the pistol back in the holster. He turned toward the back door of the saloon, then back to Jules Billings, his whole body shaking with a nameless fury. He knelt and clawed at the pants leg. No, not yet. Not here. Hide the body first.

He dragged Billings across the rocky ground to the brush that fringed the edge of the draw. Pulling the limp body behind the bushes, he collapsed and began yanking at the right pants leg. Hiking it above the boot top, he felt the pouch, groped at it until it came free. The weight was like a trophy in his hand, and he smiled.

But now what? His chest was burning as if he had run a mile at full sprint. What was he going to do with Billings? What if the prospector came around before Charlie could get his supplies in the morning? Damn, he hadn't thought about that! Maybe he should have stuck to the saloon plan. Hell, maybe he should have just broken into a store and stolen his supplies.

He looked down at Jules Billings. Tie him up? No rope. Gag him? With what? "Shit," the outlaw said.

Jules Billings groaned. A leg moved.

The outlaw Charlie Holt jumped back, pulled his pistol. No, don't shoot, he thought. Damn, what was he going to do?

The back door of the saloon opened, and a trio of laughing young men poured out. Billings groaned loud, put a hand to his head. He was trying to sit up!

Charlie's pistol came down hard on the miner's head as he heard the three men hooting. He struck old Jules again. Again, and again. He paused, then lay three more crushing licks across the battered head.

He looked toward the saloon, saw the three men standing in a row, urinating. They laughed, then set up a chorus to rival the wildest pack of timber wolves in the mountains. Old Jules Billings had been wrong. It was not his night to howl.

Twenty-one

❧

As far as Carrol Moncrief knew, he was the first and only preacher to have ever set foot in Frisco, Colorado. He enjoyed a monopoly here, and never did he need it more than today. As he trotted his tired horse into town, he found himself hoping for a prayer meeting, a funeral, a shotgun wedding—any excuse he might find to pass his hat.

It was not Sunday, so only a few miners were in town from their claims, and fewer would likely be in a frame of mind to worship. It was not even Wednesday, on which evening the Frisco Christian Society met in the vacant second story of the newspaper office. It was Thursday noon, and Frisco lay as fallow for the gleanings of a circuit preacher as it would all week.

"Now, Carrol," he said, admonishing himself. "The Lord will provide."

He rode first to the general store of Edgar Dreyer, who

served as the town's undertaker by virtue of the fact that he sold pine coffins. Carrol might have simply asked Dreyer for credit, except that he already owed the man nearly a hundred dollars. He had planned to repay Dreyer with part of the five hundred the Church of the Weeping Virgin had promised him, but Dee Hassard had destroyed even that intention.

"Howdy, Edgar," he said, stepping into the general store.

"Carrol! Goddamn, it's good to see you."

The preacher winced. "Now, Edgar, you promised me you'd work on your language."

Dreyer gritted his teeth. "Shit," he said, then clapped his hand over his mouth, his face bug-eyed. He turned to a slate behind his counter, and with a piece of chalk rock made two hash marks, one on either side of a dividing line. "Well, that's only three blasphemies and a half a dozen profanities so far today. I'm under the average, Carrol. That tally board you give me helps."

"Try a little harder, Edgar. Learn to say 'fiddlesticks' or 'dagnabbit' or somethin' that ain't so offensive." He glanced around the empty store. "How's business?"

"Slack. We need a fresh strike around here. All the diggin's are dwindlin', dagnabbit. What brings you around? Didn't expect to see you till next month."

"Some little redheaded flimflam artist stole a church from me."

Dreyer's eyes shifted. He had seen the redhead lead the strange congregation hastily through town a few days ago. "You don't mean them pilgrims, do you? The fanatics?"

"That's them. I was supposed to guide 'em into the mountains, but a fellow named Dee Hassard jumped my claim and took over the whole congregation. How long since they been through here?"

"Just three or four days. We was all hopin' they'd settle near here, maybe pick business up some, but they didn't even stop for a day. Didn't buy no supplies or nothin'. Just plowed right on through town like they was in a big hurry. I see why now, if you was after the leader."

"He was still with 'em when they came through here?"

"Yeah, a little redheaded feller."

Carrol nodded grimly. "Well, he'll probably be long gone by the time I catch up to the pilgrims, and I'm sure he'll get away with every penny they've got, too. I'll keep after him, though. He did more than cheat me out of that five hundred, Edgar. He killed my brother, Frank, down in South Park."

Dreyer's mouth dropped open, then he scowled. He snatched up his piece of chalk rock and made an angry swipe at the side of the slate designated for enumerating profanities. "Why, that son of a bitch!" he said.

Carrol looked back toward the pine boxes. "I'll allow you that one, Edgar. Got any work for me?"

"Got a feller needs buryin' back here, but I doubt anybody'll turn out to pay for you prayin' over his grave."

Carrol shuffled curiously toward the coffins, feeling drawn to one in particular with the lid on, but not nailed down yet. "Who is it?"

"Old Jules Billings. Got hisself killed last night. Somebody beat his head in."

Carrol lifted the lid, squinted his eyes a little at the shape of the dead man's head. "Any idea who?"

"He left through the back door of the Eagle Saloon last night with some stranger. Somebody found him out behind the saloon this mornin'."

"Where's the stranger?" Carrol asked, quietly lowering the lid on the coffin, as if he didn't want to disturb the man who rested within.

Dreyer shrugged. "Some of the boys looked around. We figured he hightailed it back toward Georgetown. Did you see anybody suspicious on your way up this mornin'?"

Carrol shook his head. "Didn't see anybody at all. He must have headed south for Buena Vista."

"The funny thing is, we can't figure out why this stranger killed poor ol' Jules. He wasn't robbed. Still had his watch in his pocket. He never had no money or gold, anyway. He was buyin' drinks on credit last night, just like always."

"No family?"

"Story he used to tell was that he run away from an orphanage in Alabama when he was just a kid. Claimed he stowed away around the Horn to California and got rich in forty-nine. Been prospectin' in these mountains for years. Everybody liked him, but he was sort of a crank. Did you ever hear his story about the cross?"

"What cross?" Carrol said.

"Ol' Jules claimed he got lost up in the Sawatch years ago. Wandered above the timberline and found a huge cross made out of snow on the side of a mountain. Said that's when he took religion, and found his way out of the mountains like he'd growed up there." Dreyer shook his head, chuckled, and rolled his eyes. "He was a crazy old codger."

"Don't laugh too hard, Edgar. That cross is up there. The photographer for the Hayden party made a picture of it last year. I've seen the picture myself."

Dreyer looked at the pine box and smirked. "Well, I'll be switched. I just figured Ol' Jules was stretchin' the blanket, like all them stories he told about the claims he's filed on. He was always hittin' these big mother lodes that'd play out on him. Owed everybody in town."

Carrol grunted. It wasn't much to work with, but it was something. "And everybody in town owes *him*, Edgar. If the old man was well liked, his friends ought to turn out to see him buried. Is the grave dug?"

Dreyer looked at his watch. "Should be by now, I'd say."

"Nail that coffin shut and get ready for the funeral. I expect you to sing loudest."

The preacher left the store and angled across the street toward the Eagle Saloon. Stepping in, he waited until the eyes of the seven or eight occupants were on him. "I need six men," he announced.

Boggs frowned from behind the bar when he recognized the preacher. "I've warned you about harassin' my customers, Moncrief. You leave these men alone."

Carrol ignored the bar owner. "Six men with strong backs," he said.

"What for?" a customer said.

"Pallbearers for Jules Billings."

"That's enough," Boggs said, reaching under the bar for his shotgun. "Get out while you can, or I'll fill your hind end with pellets."

Carrol Moncrief put his grip around his pistol butt, drew the weapon calmly but quickly from the holster, all the while keeping his eye on the bartender. He leveled the barrel as Boggs lifted the shotgun, let a round go into the wall before the bartender could get a thumb hooked over a hammer. "Drop it!" he ordered.

Boggs tossed the scatter gun onto the bar. "Whoa, Preacher," he said.

Carrol smiled wickedly through the smoke, turned his muzzle upward, and let another two shots fly, causing dust to rain from the ceiling. "You sinners have been neglecting your Christian duty! A good man's been killed. Murdered by one of your customers, Boggs. Everybody get up now, we're gonna have a funeral!"

The customers rose and shuffled toward the door.

"You boys go get the coffin," Carrol said.

"Yes, sir," a man replied, grinning and tipping his hat.

Boggs came around the bar, a scowl on his face. "Damn you, Moncrief, you've gone too far this time!"

Carrol clicked the cylinder of his revolver, punching out empty shells. "Where's your business sense, Boggs? We'll get half the town down to the graveyard, say a few words for Old Jules, sing a hymn, then you announce first round on the house at the Eagle Saloon. You'll have the Thursday of your career."

Boggs contemplated a moment, then smirked. "Maybe

I'll even pay off Jules's bar tab. All right, Moncrief, I'll go along this once." He shook his head as he walked out of the bar. "You're the damnedest man of the cloth I ever laid eyes on."

Carrol marched down the street in advance of the funeral procession, shouting into open doors, knocking on closed ones. It was a beautiful, warm mountain day, and for that he gave thanks. It would have been difficult herding these mourners into a muddy street. He limbered up his vocal chords as he made his way through town, railing by the time he had reached the outskirts.

Behind him, Edgar Dreyer had started a verse of "Shall We Gather at the River," which seemed appropriate, for the young Frisco cemetery lay hard by the banks of the Blue. By the time they reached the narrow hole in the ground—the grave-diggers still on hand with their picks and shovels—the procession had taken on a long trail of curious townsmen, friends of the late Jules Billings, bored merchants relishing the change in routine, busted miners anxious to forget their troubles long enough to celebrate life over the grave of one less fortunate, even a couple of weeping harlots who had known and liked old Jules.

Carrol read the Scripture loud and fast as the frothing Blue rushed by in kind. He wished the soul of poor Jules godspeed on its journey to the reward. ". . . and, God most merciful and wise," he prayed at last, his eyes welling up with real tears, "help us find it in our hearts to forgive even that cruel and wicked servant of the devil who so viciously murdered our friend. Oh, this is the greatest task you give us, Lord, for we loved Jules and will miss him. But yours is to judge, and ours is to trust in your wisdom. So be it. Amen."

Carrol Moncrief saw a tear drop on the clod of dirt he held in his hand. As the pallbearers lowered the box into the hole, he tossed the clod in, hearing it drop loudly on the planks. "Amazing Grace" was sung as the preacher stared into the grave and wept, but a few of the mourners able to blink back their tears.

It was so hard. So very hard to forgive. Carrol tried to find the forgiveness his heart. He searched and prayed for it, but it wasn't there. He hated Dee Hassard. Hated him with the ire of the devil.

Edgar Dreyer passed his hat, seeing that Carrol had forgotten, and it swelled with contributions as the last chorus was sung. Even the grave-diggers pitched in their wages.

"First round on the house at the Eagle!" Boggs shouted. "In honor of Jules Billings!"

It was later, in the store of Edgar Dreyer, that Carrol Moncrief counted the money and weighed the dust, giving most of it back to Dreyer in exchange for the supplies he needed to stay on the trail of Dee Hassard.

"You might as well have this, too," Dreyer said, handing a certificate to the preacher.

"What is it?" Carrol asked.

"A new claim Jules filed just yesterday."

"Is it worth anything?" Carrol asked.

Dreyer began to chuckle. "I wouldn't piss in the rain with a slicker on for half a dozen of Old Jules's claims. He didn't know squat about prospectin' these mountains."

Carrol put the certificate in his pocket. "There goes your language again, Edgar. You've got to try harder."

Dreyer bunched his eyebrows together and ran through what he had last said. " 'Piss' is profane?" he asked.

"Yes, it is," the preacher answered. "And offensive, too."

"I didn't know that," the store owner admitted, and apologetically made another hash mark on his slate.

Twenty-two

❧

Dee Hassard was fighting a familiar compulsion. Every time a big job got this close to the final thrust, he took an urge to grab the money and run. Somebody would be getting suspicious by this point, even if nobody showed it. Some detective or former victim might be catching up to him, for he had used the same alias too long, worked the same mark. The temptation was to take part of the loot—enough to carry him for a while—and clear out of the territory.

In this particular case, Hassard knew Elder Hopewell harbored doubts. He knew Clarence Philbrick was downright suspicious. He could feel Carrol Moncrief sniffing his ever fresher trail. But Hassard was a professional. He would plan this thing to the last beat, stick to the plan, and escape unscathed as he always did. That was what separated him from the common sneak thief.

Sure, he was nervous. A little worried, too. Nothing

wrong with that. That was what made it interesting. If anything went wrong, he could always sneak out or change the plan. He had learned to think quickly over the years. It was second nature to him by now to constantly calculate.

He had made up his mind. He was going to pull this thing off, then use Wyckoff's scam in Australia—start his own church there, rake in tens of thousands.

He had badgered enough information out of these pilgrims now that he even understood the three-day initiation. Just a bunch of preaching by the congregation members, working in relays, spelling each other in order to harangue the recruit nonstop with Christian propaganda. The key was to get the recruit to dredge up a bunch of past failures and humiliations, and then to keep repeating them as a reminder of how awful life is outside of the Church of the Weeping Virgin. It's different inside the church, of course. Give yourself to the church and you will be cared for the rest of your life, in spite of failure or humiliation.

The odd twist was that getting initiated like this automatically trained the new member in how to initiate the next recruit. And they believed it! These fanatics actually thought that this scam in the guise of a church could manufacture some kind of emotion akin to a mama's love or something.

This was really nothing new in the ancient art of the swindle. One of the easiest ways to win trust was to listen to a victim's worst experiences and act as if you gave a damn. That's all the Church of the Weeping Virgin was doing, only its members didn't even know it.

Australia was prime territory for a Weeping Virgin–style sect, and there Hassard would set up shop. It took money to get to Australia, though, and the swindler was determined to travel in style after this wilderness ordeal. He had earned it.

It was all going to have to fall into place within a couple of days, for Carrol Moncrief could not be far behind by this time. The thing Hassard needed most was something to occupy the pilgrims—a town site for the Church of the Weeping Virgin. And as he trudged around a bend in the trail, he found it.

The forest opened up to reveal a sloped clearing of about fifty acres. Near the bottom of the slope, the Eagle River shushed the wind in the mountain peaks. Around the rest of the grassy meadow grew firs, spruces, and pines. A cluster of aspens stood at the high end, their straight white trunks spaced regularly, like the teeth of an ivory comb.

It was a sight to take one's breath: the rocky, snow-streaked mountain rising above timberline in the distance. A huge bluff stood not far up the valley of the Eagle, looking like a lost precipice from some red desert canyon. High above, a hawk called, its piercing voice pricking Hassard's ears like a call to action.

A movement caught his eye across the meadow, and he made out a lone prospector striking camp along the tree line. Hassard broke into a trot, hailing the prospector as he approached.

"Howdy," he said, out of breath as he drew within earshot. This high altitude taxed his lungs. He reckoned he was close to nine thousand feet here, judging from the proximity of the timberline.

"Stop there," the miner said, swinging his rifle up.

Hassard showed his palms. "Don't want any trouble. Just wanted to talk to you before you broke camp."

The white-bearded miner spat a brown stream out of the left side of his mouth. "Well, talk, then."

"You have a claim here?"

The old man cackled. "Ain't no gold here. I'm on my way higher up."

"This place have a name?" Hassard removed his hat and slicked a sweaty strand of red hair back alongside his head.

"Utes call it Tigiwon. One of their campgrounds."

"Seen any of 'em around?"

The miner hissed, as if disgusted at the ignorance of this greenhorn. "They all went down to the Los Piños agency for their annuities. You won't see any of 'em around here for a spell."

"You know this area pretty good?"

The prospector nodded once.

"Have you heard of the Mount of the Snowy Cross?"

"Heard of it? Hell, I seen it! I seen it before them government surveyors come through here last year to photograph it. I was the first white man to lay eyes on it."

Hassard began to feel excited. This was a pilgrimage of sorts, even for him. This grueling trek was a tribute to his profession, his power over ordinary human beings, his supremacy over their silly codes and statutes. "How do you get to it?" he asked, sensing that the old prospector was anxious to leave.

The miner picked up his pack, pointed his rifle toward the snowy summit that rose behind him. "See that peak above the timber? That's called Notch Mountain. You see that notch in it, don't you? Well, you claw your way up that mountain—through the timber and across the creeks—till you get above the timberline. Then you keep goin', over the boulders and the snow fields, and you cross the divide to the south of the peak there. That's where you'll see the cross. It's a sight, son. It'll make your skin crawl." He turned his eyes back to the stranger, then squinted at something across the meadow.

Hassard looked over his shoulder and saw the ragged party of sojourners emerging from the woods. "That's my congregation," he explained. "We've come to see the cross, and to establish a town here."

The prospector sneered. "You won't see none of me no more. I'm goin' higher up." He turned his back and trudged up the trail.

"Hey!" Hassard called. He was curious now. Just curious. "How'd you ever come to find that cross in the first place?"

The old man stopped and turned to look at the stranger.

"Like the song says: 'I once was lost, but now am found.'
It's never too late, son." And he paced into the shadows,
vanishing among shafts of sunlight.

Dee Hassard shrugged and walked back toward the
center of the meadow. He stood there, cultivating an
expression of reverence to wear for the pilgrims. It
wasn't hard at this moment. He had found almost everything he needed. The town site was here, the fabled cross
just a day's hike over the ridge, the gold in one lump
on Elder Hopewell's burro. He needed only two things
now: an escape route and a way to get rid of Clarence
Philbrick.

He didn't want to have to kill that rich boy from back
east. That would make things messy. But Philbrick was
getting suspicious. The arrogant little snot thought he
knew something, thought he was too smart, too educated.
Well, there was only one way to handle a fool like that.
Put him in your hip pocket. Keep him so close to you that
he couldn't draw a breath to shout thief without you
hearing him. And if he did draw that breath, you'd better
be prepared to prevent him from ever using it.

"Are we gonna stop here for lunch?" asked a young
black man who always walked near the head of the party.

"Yes," Hassard said. "We'll have lunch here tomorrow, too. And the day after, and every day of your life."

A red-faced woman dropped her pack. "You mean this
is where we're to build?" She looked around her, mindful
for the first time today of the grandeur of the Eagle River
valley.

"We'll call the town Tigiwon," Hassard announced,
sweeping his arms. "It's a Ute word that means 'sacred
place.' " He didn't know what the word meant at all, of
course. "This is where the New Order of Christianity will
begin, and from here, spread throughout the world!"

Elder Hopewell approached, uncertain. Sure, he liked
the looks of this place. Who wouldn't relish beauty like
this? But wouldn't it get cold here in the winter?

Wouldn't the snow last for months up here? "You sure?" he said. "How come this place?"

Hassard pointed at the notch in the summit to the southwest—a groove filed in a huge rifle sight, drawing aim on the Snowy Cross. "We're just a day's hike to the cross from here. I can sense it. We're going to be free here, Elder Hopewell. Free of everything unholy!"

The young Vermonter had stopped at Hopewell's side, joining him in his reservations. "Isn't it a little high here for a permanent settlement?" he asked.

"Nearer to God," Deacon Dee replied. "Besides, I've lived in a dozen mining towns higher than this."

"But there's nothing to mine here," Clarence said. "How do you expect people to make a living here?"

Hassard looked at the Vermonter as if the boy had lost his mind. "The Utes have made their living here for a thousand years. We'll learn from the red man. Don't we have red-skinned brothers and sisters in our own congregation? We'll hunt, gather the fruits of the wilderness, cultivate our own crops for our own consumption. We need only enough to exist, brother Clarence. we don't need to produce anything for sale. *The Wisdom of the Ages* and the dreams I have had make that clear."

Looking down on them, Hassard saw that he had most of them with him in this. But there was a clutch of doubtful minds clustered around Elder Hopewell, Sister May, and the Vermonter. It was time to address the problem. Meet it head-on.

"I know that some of you doubt me," he said. "I can see it in your eyes. But the Weeping Virgin has guided me here to this spot. In my dreams I have seen a cross of pure white snow on the face of a mountain over this ridge." He thrust his finger angrily at Notch Mountain. "Tomorrow I will take a party to find it, and when you see it, then you will surely believe, and we shall wash our hands of our filthy lucre! We'll leave it in sight of the Holy Cross and begin anew! If the cross is there, you'll know!"

"Amen!" shouted one of Hassard's believers.

"Now, what does *The Wisdom of the Ages* say?" Hassard continued. "We don't have a moment to waste in this life. Let's sustain ourselves with a meal, then get to work. We'll build the church first, up there on the highest point of the meadow!"

"Hallelujah!" a woman answered.

Hassard felt a tingle travel up his spine. This preaching business agreed with him. He was going to enjoy the hell out of this once he got to Australia.

Twenty-three

❧

The sun had dropped behind Notch Mountain when Dee Hassard approached the place called Tigiwon. There were still hours of daylight left but it was cool, shadowy, like the brink of nightfall in flatter regions—a high-country phenomenon he had never gotten used to. It made him feel that time was growing short, like daylight slipping away.

Maybe it wasn't the mountain's shadow making him feel that way. Maybe it was the fact that Carrol Moncrief had to be getting closer to him by the minute.

The confidence man had ridden a big red mule a few miles up the valley, hobbled the beast there, and walked back. He had hoped to overtake that white-haired prospector he had met in the meadow, get some more details about the climb to the cross. But the old man hadn't even left any tracks. No matter. He would find the way.

It was almost as good as done now. Hassard had his
escape route planned: up the trail to Tennessee Pass on
the big red mule, down into the valley of the Arkansas, to
Buena Vista and points beyond. Everything was in place.

Everything but Clarence Philbrick. Hassard knew one
thing for certain. Tomorrow, when he announced that he
would take the gold up to the Snowy Cross for the dedication, Philbrick was going to insist on going along. The
Vermonter had appointed himself watchdog of the
church coffers.

What was he going to do about Philbrick? An accident
tonight? Too obvious. That would only arouse more suspicion. He didn't want to have to sacrifice Brother
Clarence to the Snowy Cross tomorrow. He hated that
sort of thing. Killing always made somebody hound him
harder. And besides, it was sloppy—unprofessional.

He thought back to his education under the East Coast
masters. They would say to keep Clarence in view. Know
at all times where he was, what he was doing. Yes, the
thing to do at dawn tomorrow was to *invite* Clarence to
come along before he could insist on it. That might lower
the young fool's suspicions.

Then, maybe . . . Just maybe the best plan was to leave
all that money up there on the divide, like he had been
promising to do all along. Yes, *dedicate* it! Really leave
it there and come back to the town site. That would
probably convince even Clarence. Nobody was going to
bother the money up there.

Then, in the middle of the night, when Clarence and all
the other doubters were asleep, Hassard would sneak
back up to retrieve his wages. It just might work. He
would have several hours' head start on them. He would
come down the mountain where he had left the big red
mule, and ride for Buena Vista. What a slick haul that
would be!

"That you, Deacon?" The voice came from the trail to
Tigiwon.

"Yes," Hassard said. "Just me."

The guard stepped into the open path, a burly youth with a single-shot squirrel gun.

"Good job," Hassard said, grasping the guard by the shoulder. "We must all stay alert, even in this wilderness, Brother . . ."

"James. James O'Rourke."

He patted the muscled shoulder. "I don't expect we'll have anybody bothering us a way out here, but you know what Pastor Wyckoff used to say: 'Prepare! For the devil lurks in the guise of Godliness!' "

"Yes," Brother James said. "What happened to your mule?"

Hassard began to laugh. "I was trotting up the trail, beholding the beauty of God's creations all around me, when that blessed creature ran me right under a tree limb. I landed on my rear end, and Ol' Red just kept trotting away. But, what did God give me legs for?"

"You want me to go catch the mule?"

"You have a more important job here. Don't worry about Ol' Red. He'll wander back to Tigiwon in a day or two." He smiled at the young guard and strode on toward the town site. "Hone your eyesight," he said. "I'll see you tonight in Tigiwon."

He loved that name. He loved the way these people looked up to him. This could be infectious. When he thought about it, Wyckoff's scam seemed to be one that actually benefited the victims. These people were like sheep. Hell, they begged to be swindled. He hoped he would find plenty just like them in Australia. But then, there was no need to worry about that. There were fools like this everywhere.

"You should have known Pastor Wyckoff in the old days," Hopewell said. He paused just long enough to straighten, sop the sweat from his eyebrows, and to glance at the beauty of the long-shadowed mountain slope.

Clarence and May helped him roll the log they were peeling for the new church.

"That character sure had a way with words," Clarence said, "judging from his book." The construction of this church was a ridiculous thing to him, but he was helping in order to stay close to May. Hunting had gone well since he killed that first buck, and he had some time to burn before the evening hunt.

"Oh, you should have heard Pastor Wyckoff preach," Hopewell replied. "He could hold a group breathless—I mean really breathless, to where they wouldn't even risk making a sound to breathe for fear they might miss him whisper. Then he'd roar something at them, and they'd bolt up like lightning struck them."

"Fast talk and leadership don't always amount to the same thing."

"You're skeptical," Hopewell said. "That's understandable. I was, too, even after I heard Pastor Wyckoff speak. Then I went through the initiation. That's when I realized that the Church of the Weeping Virgin was going to be God's salvation to the world. Give us a fair chance, Clarence. Consider joining the church."

Clarence snorted. "I'm not interested."

"Why not?"

"This initiation. Nobody in your congregation will tell me anything about it. They all act as if they know something I don't. Like they're flaunting it; proud of it; selfish with it. It's all too secretive and elitist for me. Everything I ever learned about faith is based on truth, light. Not darkness."

Hopewell shook his head. "I know it's hard to understand if you haven't experienced it. I wish you could talk to Pastor Wyckoff. He could convince you. We had true leadership when he was alive."

"What about you?" May said quickly. She could feel the religious conflict deepening between Hopewell and Clarence and didn't like the thought of them being at odds with each other. "You got the church from Arkansas to Denver after Wyckoff was lynched." She flaked a large piece of bark off with her draw knife and moved on down the log. "You could lead them as well as anybody."

The tall man straightened again, rising to his full height. He was standing above them on the slope, and he looked like one of the straight trees the pilgrims were felling in the forest, tall and slender, his white hair and whiskers like bundles of moss. "I'm no match for the likes of Pastor Wyckoff. I don't have his use of words."

"This rabble would be better off with you leading them than Dee Hassard," Clarence said.

"He's got a way of whipping people in behind him," Hopewell replied. "He's not as good with speech as Pastor Wyckoff was, but he's handy at it. He's got me worried. I can't say just why, but I think it has something to do with the money."

"You mean throwin' it away up on that mountain?" May said.

The elder nodded. "Pastor Wyckoff never had any objection to the church making or keeping money. To him, money was like this ax." He held the broad iron blade in front of him, a long arm's length away. "It can be a good tool, if you use it properly, the way it is intended. It can also be used to crush somebody's skull. It has nothing to do with any amount of holiness or evil in the instrument itself, but in the user. Same with money."

Clarence nodded. "I agree." He looked toward his jacket, which was lying within his grasp under his Remington rifle. "Same with guns. They can be used for protection or aggression. But if the aggressor's got one, the protector had better have one, too."

"A sad truth," Hopewell said. "One we have learned."

They worked the log in silence for a few moments, hearing the cadence of axes in the forest above them.

"What about Hassard's guns?" May said. "Have you noticed? That little pistol he wears tucked under his belt looks like it's been lying out somewhere in the weather.

Then he's got that big pistol in that holster, all shiny and polished, and the gun belt has a new hole poked in it because whoever owned it before Hassard was bigger around than him."

Clarence contemplated, impressed by what she had said. He didn't know what it meant any more than May did, but there was something wrong with the deacon's whole getup. "Everything about him is suspect. Who is he, anyway? He says Reverend Moncrief sent him, but how are we to know?" He paused, looked up toward Notch Mountain. "I'm going with him when he takes the party to find the cross."

"I intend to go, too," Hopewell said. "But we'd better be careful. We'd better watch him every second."

"Clarence," May said. "What if there really is a cross up there?"

The Vermonter smiled. "The cross exists."

Elder Hopewell stopped with his ax above one shoulder and looked at the hunter.

Clarence nodded. "I've seen a photograph of it, taken last summer by a photographer for the U.S. geological survey. I don't know how Hassard found out about it, but it is just as he described it."

Hopewell lowered the ax. "Why didn't you say something?"

Clarence searched the ground, as if for reason. "I'm not sure. I felt there was some kind of advantage to my keeping quiet about it.

"There's something strange about all this. From the moment I saw that photograph, I knew I would climb Notch Mountain someday to see that cross. It was one of the final things that made me know I had to come west. I had planned to get situated in New Mexico first. It was only by chance that I met May, and we fell in with the Church of the Weeping Virgin. It's almost as if I were destined to come here—drawn here like some beast on a migratory journey." The Vermonter was virtually reciting the entry he would make in his diary that night.

A rifle blast suddenly ripped the wide-open air above the meadow. Axes fell silent, the rush of the river and the echo of the gunshot the only remaining strains. Clarence picked up his Remington, swung an arm into his jacket sleeve, and trotted toward the sound of the shot, on the trail that led north down the river valley. He ran into the timber flanking the trail below Tigiwon and soon saw a guard matching toward the town site—a lanky, rawboned man stalking angrily in front of him, his hands in the air.

"What's this?" Clarence asked.

The guard was named Dan Feather, a Kickapoo who had joined the church in Indian Territory. He had the stranger's gun belt slung across one shoulder. "He no stop," Dan said, "so I shoot."

"Who are you?" Clarence said to the man.

"Charlie Holt. I come for my wife."

"Your wife?"

Dan Feather scowled. "He want Sister May."

Twenty-four

❧

May waited with Elder Hopewell, watching the open slope, trying to eke some sound out of the air. Below, to her right, she saw Dee Hassard trot into the opening. Seconds later, along the left side, a sight emerged from the forest that struck her with sudden terror.

"What is it?" Hopewell said, hearing her gasp.

She saw Clarence appear behind her husband. The Vermonter's eyes found hers immediately, even across the distance up the slope. They questioned her, and she knew she should have told him. Charlie Holt's eyes found her next, and he pointed accusingly. She put her hand over her mouth and felt choked with fear. She was his wife. They were going to make her go back with him.

"Sister May," Hopewell said. "Who is that?"

"My husband," she said.

"May!" Charlie Holt's voice rattled up the slope. "You come on down here. I'm takin' you home!"

The elder put his long flat hand across May's shoulders. "You stay here. I'll go see into this. Don't you worry, I won't let any harm come to you."

May took some comfort from his words, but good Elder Hopewell didn't know Charlie. She turned her eyes away from her husband and sat on the log she had been peeling, dread coursing through her like a fever.

Dee Hassard met the three men in the meadow and motioned for Dan Feather to lower his weapon. This was a relief. He had thought, when he heard the shot, that Carrol Moncrief might have caught up. He didn't see how that was possible. He had calculated the distances over and over. Moncrief would come hard, but couldn't possibly get here for a couple of days yet. For all he knew, though, this character might be some detective hired by a former victim, some bounty hunter, or a friend of Frank Moncrief's. He would have to be ready and stay alert.

"State your business," he said to the stranger as he strode to the group.

"I come after my wife," Holt said, and he pointed at May again.

Hassard's eyes flashed, and he glanced at Clarence, relishing the tortured look on the hunter's face. His mind raced. May was a runaway. There was opportunity here somewhere. This was some way to get rid of Philbrick and yet build himself in the eyes of the congregation. But how? "Would you like to join our congregation?" he asked, buying time to think, knowing well that this enraged husband harbored no spiritual bent.

"Hell, no," Charlie said, the taste of whiskey thickening his tongue. "I come to take her home, damn it." He glared at the gangling black man striding down the slope.

Hassard was racing back through the gospel according to Wyckoff. He wanted more than anything to give Sister May to this stranger. Clarence would follow, and he would be rid of him. But he had to consider what *The Wisdom of Ages* would say on the matter. This was no time to lose the confidence of the pilgrims. It took him only a moment to form the policy. "Sister May is a member of our family now. You can't take her from us against her will."

Holt fumed. "She's my wife, goddammit!"

"By the laws of an unholy government that we don't recognize. Now leave, and take your foul language and your blasphemies elsewhere."

"The hell I will," Holt said, and he started up the slope, pushing Hopewell aside. "I'm takin' my wife home."

Hassard flung his coattail aside, pressed his palm against the butt of the big Colt, and drew the weapon smoothly from the belt scabbard. He cocked and aimed, flexing his trigger finger as the irons settled on the crown of Holt's hat.

The outlaw Charlie Holt shrank to the ground like a quail when he heard the report and felt the bullet rip through his hat. "Damn you!" he said.

"Brother Clarence, you can let Sister May know that everything's all right now. This man won't come back if he knows what's good for him."

Clarence hesitated. "You want help with him?"

Hassard shook his head. "Don't need it." He looked at Dan Feather. "Was he mounted?"

The Kickapoo nodded and pointed his chin down the valley. "His horse down yonder."

"I'll escort him back to his horse alone. I want to have a word with him as he leaves." Hassard waved his pistol toward the trail the stranger had arrived on. "Come on," he said.

Holt scowled but obeyed and paced long into the forest. As he passed, Hassard took Holt's gun belt from Dan Feather's shoulder.

Clarence watched them disappear, then walked slowly up the slope toward May. Facing her was going to be awkward. He had thought he was beginning to know her well until her husband showed up. Now she seemed a complete stranger. She had kept secrets from him. This wasn't some trifling thing, either. It could have gotten him killed, judging from the look on Charlie Holt's face down there.

As he came to the place where she sat, she avoided looking at him and fidgeted in her embarrassment.

"He's gone," Clarence said. He waited for a reply, but she gave none. "He said you were his wife." His tone was rather accusing.

She nodded. "I don't want to go back with him." She looked at him, her eyes full. "I know I should have told you about him, but I didn't know how." Tears poured down from her eyes, streaked her cheeks. "Please don't let him take me back."

Clarence felt suddenly ashamed. Secrets? Wasn't he carrying a few up his own sleeves? She had been no less honest with him than he had been with her. He sat down beside her and put a hand on her shoulder. "You don't have to go anywhere you don't want to," he promised. "I'll see to that."

The axes began to chop again as they sat there.

Clarence didn't know anymore if he would ever get to the Ojo de los Brazos. Could it possibly possess more beauty than the Eagle River valley of Colorado? How long could he carry this money around in his jacket? Why had this Mount of the Snowy Cross interfered with his plans? Why did he feel this way for this woman?

I once heard of two fishermen—he thought this, thinking again of the night's journal entry—who entangled their flies just as a fish struck, and both anglers hooked the selfsame trout. As one would not yield to the other, neither was able to properly play the fish, who threw both hooks and swam free.

I am that trout. The Ojo de los Brazos pulls me one way; May Tremaine another. The lures they use are diabolical. Perhaps neither shall keep me in her creel.

Twenty-five

❧

I wonder what he wants," May said. She stood beside an ancient fir, wringing her hands nervously.

Clarence shrugged. "Curious, isn't it? I mean, that he would ask both of us to meet him here."

She nodded.

The Vermonter looked up the huge trunk of the tree and decided to change the subject. "How old do you think this tree is?"

May noticed the old valley monarch beside her for the first time, its trunk rising in tons of timber. "I don't know," she said.

"I'll bet it's seen a dozen generations come and go."

She smiled a little and wondered what made a man think such thoughts. He was different from anybody she had ever known. She wanted her own mind to work the way his did. She wanted to question things, study them. She had always been too occupied with survival to think of such things. But Clarence made her feel safe and let her mind run.

"Did you ever finish that book? *The Wisdom of the Ages*?"

"Yes."

"What did you think?"

"I think that old Pastor Wyckoff was a little touched."

Clarence chuckled and nodded at her in approval. It was good that she was able to question those religious ramblings. "What about joining the Church of the Weeping Virgin?"

"They keep pestering me about it, but I don't want to go off in the woods for three days with a bunch of strangers."

"Then don't."

"They keep putting the pressure on me heavier all the time. I don't think they'll let me stay on with them if I don't join up. I don't have much choice."

"You can come with me to New Mexico. I'll see that you get situated."

May felt almost embarrassed, almost as if she had maneuvered him into saying what she wanted to hear. "Thank you, Clarence. But Charlie will be out there looking for me, and he's some put out."

"You must have had a good reason for leaving him. I've got an idea what it was, and I don't blame you. If a man hurts a woman, he doesn't deserve to be called a husband. Don't you worry about anything. If you want to go, we'll go."

They heard boots scraping a gravelly stretch of trail and turned to see Dee Hassard coming from the town site.

"Good evening," he said, "thanks for meeting me here. Let's walk up the trail a little way. I want to talk to the two of you."

It was near dusk now, the valley darkening into shades of deep blue and purple. Clarence shrugged at May, and they followed Hassard up the trail at a stroll.

"I wanted to talk to the two of you about your future with the church. You joined this party together, and you've spent much time together since you've been with us." He grinned coyly at them. "I was wondering what your plans are now."

Clarence wrinkled his brow, wondering what the deacon was up to. He propped his rifle barrel on his shoulder. "I haven't made up my mind what I'm going to do."

"Me neither," May added quickly. She was making sure to keep Clarence between her and Hassard.

They came to the picket line, and James O'Rourke stepped into the trail ahead of them. "Evenin', Deacon," the guard said.

"Are you still on guard duty, Brother James?" Hassard replied. "I'm going to send somebody to relieve you as soon as I get back to Tigiwon."

"I don't mind," the youth replied.

"We're going to walk up the trail a way, but we'll be back directly."

James nodded, and the three continued their stroll.

"I was hopin' to help you both make up your minds," Hassard said. "Brother Clarence, we'll need a hunter with a good rifle until we get crops and herds established. I owe you an apology for doubting your hunting ability before. You were right; there just wasn't any game back among the mining settlements. Here you've kept plenty of meat hanging.

"And, May, about the other day, you understand that I was suspicious about your past and just tryin' to coax some information out of you. I had the feelin' you were on the run from something. I thought maybe it was the law. But I understand, now that I've met Charlie Holt."

Clarence glanced at May, for she had said nothing about that of which Hassard now spoke.

"By the way, I warned him about ever returning for you, Sister May. I believe I put a righteous fear into him."

"He's gonna come back," May said, a grim certainty in her voice. "If he followed me this far, I know he'll keep tryin'. He's gone downright wild. I could see it in his eyes."

Hassard shrugged. "I've doubled the guard below Tigiwon, just in case."

Clarence noticed movement on the trail ahead and saw Charlie Holt step from the trees with a drawn revolver. His rifle barrel was over his shoulder, and he knew better than to swing it into action, for Holt had murder in his drunken eyes. All he could do was step in front of May.

Hassard gasped when he saw Holt. He was truly surprised. Holt was supposed to fire in ambush a good half mile up the trail. He wasn't supposed to show himself. He wasn't supposed to be this close to the guards. Already the fool had botched the plan, and Hassard knew he would have to make drastic changes. "Holt!" he said, stopping in his tracks. "You're making a big mistake."

"She's the one made it," Holt said. "You never should have run from me, woman. Never should have laid me out for good with that poker."

"It was the fryin' pan," May said, her voice less timid than even she could explain.

"Shut up and step out from behind that boy, or I'll kill you all."

Clarence used his free arm to hold May behind him. "Put your gun away," he ordered. He could think of only one thing. He had to take control. This helplessness was death. His trigger finger slipped inside the guard, his thumb found the hammer. Now, quickly, he thought, before your fear overcomes you.

May had never seen Charlie like this, and she instinctively knew it meant the worst. This was her fault. She had led him here. She was going to make something happen. She wasn't going to watch him shoot Clarence Philbrick down. No time to think. Just act!

Clarence felt May bolt to the right side of the trail, saw Charlie Holt's eyes and gun muzzle follow her. He slung the long, heavy barrel of the Remington over his shoulder without thinking, and Charlie Holt reacted, covering him with the pistol. The hammer latched as the forestock hit his left palm, and he tensed, seeing the pistol barrel swinging toward him. Dee Hassard was diving for the trees to the left as Clarence jerked the trigger, knowing he had fired too soon, over Holt's head.

He scrambled to his left, and his boot slipped. The Colt pistol fired, only shattering a dead tree limb on the ground six feet away. Clarence took cover, thought about reloading the single-shot hunting rifle. Why wasn't Hassard firing, protecting May? Holt had missed him badly. The man was no *pistolero*. No time to reload the rifle. It was going to happen too fast. Holt would have May in seconds.

He stepped back into the trail, saw Holt peering into the forest for May. He ran at the outlaw, his rifle gripped tight in both hands. The Colt pistol swung on him again, but he pushed the heavy hunting piece ahead of him—hurled it sidewise at Holt with all the force his solid arms could gather.

The rifle hit Charlie Holt's forearm, spoiled his aim as he fired. Clarence collided with him as Holt cocked the weapon for another shot. He grabbed the outlaw's wrist as they slammed against the rocky trail. The heavy jacket constricted him, and Holt was stronger than he had expected, but he held his own, and now he knew Hassard would have to do something. Or would he? Who was this Dee Hassard? Where was he now?

Hassard cursed Charlie Holt from the deepest center of his guts. This should have been so simple that he figured even an amateur like Holt could pull it off. Hassard had done everything he was supposed to do. He had come up the trail at the right moment, stood far enough away from Clarence. Holt was supposed to kill the Vermonter, grab the girl, and ride like hell before the guards could come. But he had shown his face, and he had set his ambush too close to the guards, and now they were coming. Holt might talk.

Hassard drew his Colt and ran for the two men on the ground. They made a good match—about the same size, and both of them strong: Holt from farm labor, Philbrick from a rich boy's calisthenics. He was hoping this wouldn't look too obvious. Thank goodness he had raised all that talk about their future with the church— just in case something like this went wrong.

He could hear James O'Rourke's footsteps coming up the dim trail as he landed on the two men. His left hand grabbed Holt's gun, as if to aid Clarence. The muzzle of his own pistol pressed against Holt's chest. He saw Holt release Clarence's jacket—a strange look of fear and curiosity in his bloodshot eyes. Hassard listened to three of O'Rourke's foot beats, then fired.

May Tremaine screamed and sprang from the trees. She saw Clarence roll away from her husband as the bloody outlaw's eyes rolled toward her and locked onto her, staring forever.

Hassard sprang to his feet and dropped his revolver as if it were hot. "I had to shoot him," he said. "He was reachin' for my gun. He could have killed Clarence. He could have killed me." He was explaining this to James O'Rourke, who would take the news back to Tigiwon— James O'Rourke, who was posturing excitedly over the dead man with his weapon.

Clarence stepped over the outlaw Charlie Holt, breaking the death stare that held May. He glanced sideways at Hassard, who had handled everything poorly. Today in the meadow called Tigiwon, Hassard had acted swiftly and effectively, firing through Holt's hat. Here he had waited too long, then acted too rashly. Clarence had pinned Holt. The guard was coming. There was no need to kill the man.

He grabbed May's arm to lead her away, when, unexpectedly, she pulled her arm from his grasp and gripped his wrist instead. He found her looking at him as no

woman ever had, and something indomitable came clear
between them. She was tired of being weak, and he was
making her strong.

"Wait," she said. "His things are mine. I'm his next
of kin."

Clarence watched, amazed, as she knelt to unbuckle
the gun belt from Charlie Holt's hips. She dragged the
leather out from under the body, then took the pistol from
the limp hand. She holstered the Colt, handed it to
Clarence, then looked back at James O'Rourke. "Anything else he has, the church can own."

There was no Charlie Holt behind her now, and she
wanted nothing more than to leave this place with the
tall Vermonter. Yet it wasn't that simple with Clarence,
and she knew it. He had arrived at a personal struggle
with the man who claimed to be a deacon. It was as if
they were arm-wrestling or something, and now they
were growing weary of the contest and both desirous of
an end.

She looked at them both, and they knew—they all
three knew. They couldn't speak it, or even speak of it,
yet it was there to resolve. Someone would have to prove
something tomorrow.

Ramon looked at Sister Petra's face, her features aglow
in the soft firelight. How could she sleep? He was too
excited to even lie down, let alone sleep. They had met
an old prospector who had seen the Mount of the Snowy
Cross. Seen it with his own eyes! Ramon hadn't understood a word of his speech, but Petra had translated. This
was the old prospector who had been spoken of in Buena
Vista. That they should even cross his path was a miracle
in itself.

He pulled his wool blanket tighter against his neck and
it scratched his skin. It was cold here at night and always
a bit musty smelling. He tried to imagine how warm it
was in Guajolote right now. That was a wonderful place
to sleep in the summertime—sleep with the windows

open and the mountain breezes flowing down clean and dry from the pine forests. Maybe that little village was worth saving. Maybe the money to buy the Ojo de los Brazos grant would drop from heaven tomorrow.

He shook his head to rid it of such ridiculous thoughts. And yet, hadn't that old prospector told them of a ragged band of pilgrims camped several miles down the valley? A party of religious fanatics come to see the cross. It was fantastic. Sister Petra was not alone in her quest for this cross. There was something to it all, and he could not fight back the feeling that something wonderful was going to happen tomorrow.

Once he had been a normal boy, unconcerned with the prospect of anything happening to his village. It seemed like such a long time ago that he had been swept up by these wild happenings and carried along on this journey almost like a twig in a river. It had been only a matter of weeks, but he had changed so much and so rapidly that he didn't know how to measure it.

He was a small boy in a land of huge mountains, and he felt helplessly insignificant sitting by the campfire tonight. That he was here seemed almost an accident. This was a journey for more important souls than his own. He had contributed nothing, and in fact had burdened Petra as much as he had aided her.

Perhaps tomorrow he could atone for it. It was to be his last chance. The old Anglo prospector had assured them that the view of the cross was only a half day's climb up the mountain. Tomorrow he was going to climb as he never had before. And if he had to carry Sister Petra on his back to see that cross, he was going to do it.

He forced himself to lie back on his bed of spruce boughs. Sleep, Ramon, he said to himself. Sleep, you idiot. You must show your strength tomorrow. It is your last chance.

Twenty-six

❧

Hassard rose from the log where he had eaten his breakfast of venison steak and saw the eyes of several hopeful pilgrims following him as he reached for the coffeepot over the fire. They had risen to breakfast with him under the stars, in hopes that he might choose them to accompany him up the mountain.

He was getting anxious now. The time was near when he would have to deal with Brother Clarence.

He had Philbrick figured: Over educated and over confident. Morally responsible and physically formidable. A simpleton in terms of practical experience. His ideas of fair play would prove his downfall. He really had no inkling how far Dee Hassard would go. It might have been possible to dupe young Clarence before last night. But the Charlie Holt affair had taught him something. The boy had instincts that he was just too educated to know how to use yet. He would probably never get the chance.

Less than twenty-four hours from now, Hassard was going to leave this camp and head back up the mountain to retrieve the loot that he would leave there today. Philbrick would probably be watching him, waiting for him, and he would have to make silent work of the young Vermonter. This was the reason that Hassard now carried Charlie Holt's dagger. He disliked using knives, but it would have to be done. He would kill Clarence if he had to, get the money from the divide, locate the hobbled mule he had left up the valley, and ride for Buena Vista a half day ahead of Carrol Moncrief.

Carrol Moncrief: Dangerous. Vengeful. Possessed with affecting the capture or death of Dee Hassard. Weakness: Religious scruples. Yet, Moncrief had seen this side of the law. He might easily revert. It was imperative to stay beyond the big preacher's reach. The man was already mounted and riding by this time in the morning and would be at Tigiwon by noon tomorrow, no sooner. It was time to wrap this thing up.

He looked across the camp at the faces of the congregation. They were watching him so expectantly. Oh, glory, what a life to lead! To think that these wretched pilgrims would resign themselves to hard labor and prayer. He hated them. They were small, stupid, and gullible. They would only get what they deserved.

"I had another dream last night," he said, low and thoughtfully, warming his cup of coffee with a splash from the pot. "A visitation."

"From the Weeping Virgin?" someone asked.

Hassard nodded. "She gave me specific instructions to follow today, and I am afraid they will disappoint many of you. I don't understand why I am to do this, I only know I must."

"Do what?" Clarence asked. He was wearing the Colt revolver of the late Charlie Holt.

"I am forbidden to touch the money that we are to

dedicate to the Snowy Cross today. Instead, I am to take a small party of faithful with me to carry the stuff and accompany me to the cross."

A murmur swept around the fire as the pilgrims shuffled uncomfortably.

"In days to come, you will all see it," Hassard insisted reassuringly. "I'm sure we'll make regular pilgrimages to it. It's the personal experience for each of you that counts, not who gets to go first. But today, I am to take only a few."

"How many?" James O'Rourke asked. He was certain that Hassard would include him, now that they were personally acquainted after yesterday's trouble.

"Three. The first is Elder Hopewell. The second is Sister Mary Whitepath. The third, Brother Clarence."

O'Rourke sprang to his feet. "What about me? I joined the church in Baltimore, before any of them, except Elder Hopewell!"

"I can't explain why these have been chosen," Hassard said. "I can't even explain why I have been chosen. I, too, joined the church after you, Brother James, only as recently as Denver. I only know what the Weeping Virgin has told me." He shrugged apologetically. "Try to remember what Pastor Wyckoff has written about personal sacrifice. Perhaps this is yours."

O'Rourke sat sullenly down against a tree trunk.

Dee Hassard picked up a hatchet and felt its edge with his thumb. "Elder Hopewell. The money."

"It's here," the elder said, lifting a heavily laden saddlebag. In it were all the monies Pastor Wyckoff had collected since the pilgrimage began, plus Dee Hassard's take from the diamond field fraud, and even a bag of gold dust recovered from the body of the outlaw Charlie Holt. No one had bothered to add it all up.

"Let's go," Hassard said, rapping his coffee cup upside down on a rock to knock the dregs out. "We've got several miles to climb."

In the dark, Clarence brushed by May as he turned up

the trail. He squeezed her cool neck gently in his hand as he passed. And she touched him, too—her open palm pressing against the back of his hand, where she knew he would feel it, her fingers slipping away as he walked on.

"I'll carry the heavy stuff," Clarence said to Hopewell.

The elder handed the saddlebags to Clarence, then picked up a coil of rope and looped it over his head and one shoulder.

Mary Whitepath fell in behind them, her moccasins treading silently on supple blades of grass.

"Deacon Dee!"

The con man turned to look at James O'Rourke.

"God go with you," the youth said.

Dee smiled. "Bless you, James." With his hatchet he chopped a slash mark on an aspen tree—the first in a long line that would lead him back to the gold after today's sunset.

Sister Petra could look down and see last night's camp far below, the light of dawn showing the wisp of smoke rising through the pines. The sun hadn't even risen above the mountains to the east and already she had climbed a half mile. Her muscles were warm, the stiffness from the bed of spruce boughs gone.

Ramon was on her heels. "What are you waiting for?" he asked.

"Just looking down on the camp. We must not start too fast. We will have a long way to climb today." She smiled, for it was a joy to see him this excited about reaching the cross.

"We must not go too slow, either," he argued. "We don't know what we might run into."

They had found a game trail not far above their camp, but it had played out quickly, and now they were simply clawing their way up the steep slope, crawling under low limbs, over deadfalls and boulders. They couldn't see Notch Mountain for the trees, but knew it loomed over them, reaching high above the timber.

They worked upward for an hour, finally arriving at a minor ridge that branched off the main divide like a rib from a backbone. Working their way along the top of the ridge, they could move with relative ease among the trees, until they came to the broad flank of the mountain, where they had to negotiate steep grades again.

"Which way should we go?" Ramon asked.

Petra put her hands on her hips and saw her breath form a cloud in front of her. It was a wonderful day, sunny and warming. "The old man yesterday said to cross the Notch Mountain divide south of its summit. I think if we turn northward here and work our way gradually up the mountain as we go, we should come out above timber in about the right place."

Ramon nodded, took the lead. He didn't know why, but he felt like climbing today. His legs almost ached to be used. "Come on," he said.

Coming around a forested bluff some time later, Ramon stopped and could only stare as Petra came to his side. An avalanche had swept down the mountainside in front of him, carrying trees and rocks downward in what must have been an incredible spectacle as it occurred. Now it was nothing more than an ugly scar to cross, the footing treacherous for some sixty yards.

"I suppose we could climb and go over it," Petra said.

Ramon looked up the old avalanche. It was a long way in the wrong direction. "Look," he said pointing to a place not far above. "There's a path that some mountain sheep or something has been using."

Petra sounded nervous. "Yes, but could we?" One misplaced step could send either of them sliding hundreds of feet down the loose slope.

"One step at a time," Ramon said.

He climbed to the path the wild sheep had made and stepped onto it, testing every footfall for security. Stride by stride, he began crossing the landslide, pausing only once in the middle as a flash of something below caught his eye. He looked far downward and saw the sun reflecting in a beaver pond maybe two miles away. The avalanche had cleared a swath down through the timber, opening an incredible vista.

"Gracias a Dios," he muttered, taking in the eagle's view. Turning, he saw a look of wild terror in Sister Petra's eyes and knew he had better not ask her to look down. He moved steadily across the rest of the landslide, waiting for her on safe ground, offering his hand.

They spoke nothing, but moved on, ever upward, across the steep forested face of the mountain. Coming around another huge wrinkle in the topography, they heard water rushing not far away. As they got nearer, it grew to a roar, and soon they found the stream thundering over a precipice in a white froth.

They had to climb to get to the top of the waterfall, where slick stepping stones led them across the torrent of snowmelt. Ramon went first, leaping from one rock to the next with perfect balance. When he turned, he saw Petra still waiting across the stream.

"Come on!" he cried.

She answered, but the sound of the cascade swallowed her words. Uncertainly, she started, looking long at each successive step, gathering herself for the long stride repeatedly before chancing it. On the fifth stone, her foot slipped. The water was knee deep, cold, and swift enough to take her foot out from under her.

Ramon was in the stream in an instant, splashing toward the little nun, even though the current lacked the force to sweep her far toward the brink of the waterfall. He grabbed her by the arm and pulled her across the stream.

"I'm all right," she said. She sat down at the water's edge and caught her breath. "I didn't know it would be this hard. We've crossed nothing like this." Her eyes, for the first time since leaving Guajolote, showed her doubts.

Ramon rose and stepped back, aghast. *"Oiga,"* he ordered. "Listen to me, Sister Petra. Day after day I have followed you north looking for this cross. Now we are only a couple of miles away, and you are losing your nerve?"

"I haven't lost my nerve," she snapped. "I just didn't know it would get this dangerous. "I'm afraid one of us is going to fall off this mountain."

"Well, it's not going to be me," he said. "I'm going to find that cross. I'm going to see something that only a handful of people have ever seen. Do you want me to tell you about it, or do you want to come with me?"

Petra gritted her teeth as she rose. Something had come over this boy. How much he had changed since Guajolote. Giving orders now! *"Listo,"* she said. "I am ready," and the determination in her eyes convinced Ramon.

They trudged on at a steady grind, their legs falling into a slow rhythm. Taking a severe angle up the mountain, they covered ground more slowly, but gained altitude faster. Patches of snow began to appear in shady places, the patches growing larger as they ascended. It took thousands of wordless steps, their path wending among many obstacles of stone and wood, before they reached the timberline.

It came suddenly, the bright openness glaring down at them after the shadows of the forest. Petra looked for a path, but, of course, there was none. Ahead lay fields of snow, ancient rock slides.

"Is this Notch Mountain?" Ramon said. "Where is the notch?"

"We can't see it from here. We are too close to it. It all looks different when you are upon it."

It was cooler up here, but the sun was shining brightly, and the climb had kept them warm.

"It should be easier now," Ramon suggested. "No more dead trees to climb over."

"Yes," she answered. "But there will be more snow. We are going to have to go through it in some places. We still have a mile to climb, maybe two."

He took some dried meat from his coat pocket and

began to chew on it as he led the way up the slippery alpine tundra. He stepped in a mushy spot where melted snow had seeped and felt the cold water almost immediately on his toes. His boots were worn out from the long journey. Petra's were in better shape, and they were high-topped lace-up boots. Ramon's were low, wide-mouthed boots. They would not serve him well if he had to cross fields of snow.

Petra looked northward and saw white clouds on some far-distant range. "I hope the clouds don't gather here. It would obscure the cross."

"You worry too much. We are almost there. What could happen now?" But Ramon was worried, too. Not about whether they would find the cross, but about what would happen then. Did she really think they would find money lying around on the rocks? This trip was meant to save Guajolote. Did she remember that? How was this Snowy Cross going to save a tiny village hundreds of miles away? Petra was in for a disappointment. That was all there was to it. And she was going to be hell to live with all the way home.

Twenty-seven

❧

This was the way Frank had done it. Years ago, when Carrol was the outlaw on the run, Frank had caught up to him unexpectedly at a cabin in the San Juan Mountains. Carrol had stolen a couple of dozen cattle, shooting and wounding a cowboy who had given chase. He knew the law—probably his own brother—would trail him, so he had ridden like the devil's own jockey for Arizona, stealing fresh mounts along the way.

He had come to the abandoned cabin in Ute country, probably the former home of some long-dead fur trapper. He had chanced a few hours of sleep there, knowing that no one could have ridden harder than he had.

And yet, not three hours later, Frank Moncrief burst into the cabin and clubbed his surprised brother over the head with the barrel of a navy Colt. It was weeks later that Frank explained how he had done it. They were camped by the Platte River in South Park, on the road to the state penitentiary in Cañon City. The same place where Frank would later die at the hands of Dee Hassard.

"Bet you wonder how I caught up to you in the San Juans, don't you?" Frank had said, the gurgles of the Platte keeping time with the cracklings of the fire.

Carrol had wondered, all right. There was no way any man could have ridden harder than he had after stealing those cattle and shooting that cowboy. But he wasn't going to give Frank the satisfaction of asking how.

"You were slippin' away from me," Frank admitted. "I was ridin' hard, but I had to trail you, and that slowed me down. Every time I'd get to where you had stole a fresh horse, I was a little further behind you. I had to try somethin'.

"So when I came to that ranch you stole your last horse from, I borrowed six fresh mounts. I tied 'em in a string, head to tail, rode the lead horse till he was near dead, then switched to the next one back. Every time I did that, I'd leave the jaded horse where I'd finished with him and take the fresher horses on. I knew you were headin' for Arizona, so I just rode. Didn't worry about trailin' you anymore. I was lucky to find that cabin. Spotted the smoke from the chimney. You never should have lit that fire."

Carrol had spat on the ground between himself and his brother and said, "I'll be damned if you'll catch me next time."

"Let me promise you somethin', brother," Frank had replied, the cold glare of determination filling his eyes. "When you get out of prison, if you decide to step back on that outlaw trail, I don't care if I have to kill every horse in Colorado. I will ride you down again. If you gallop all the way to South America, I will dog you like a hound on a damned coyote."

"You do, and I'll kill you," Carrol said, and he had meant it.

Thank God it hadn't come to that. He had found a new way, in prison of all places. He had learned to place

Frank in higher regard than any man he knew. But now Frank was dead, and he was closing fast on his killer, Dee Hassard.

He was glad now that he knew about the string of horses that Frank had used to catch him years ago. The method was working well here, because the pilgrims left such a plain trail. Carrol could read it at a gallop. It was dangerous, though. Six galloping horses in a string was a wreck looking for a place to happen, and he had been happy just to drop the first tired horse from the head of the string ten miles out of Frisco.

He was down to two horses now, having lathered four mounts to near exhaustion. The last two were hardly fresh. They had run all the way from Frisco, yet they had carried no man upon their backs, felt no cinch tighten around their barrels. Each horse would carry him about five miles before tiring. If he didn't overtake the pilgrims by then, Hassard was as good as gone.

It was odd that Frank had used any horse this hard, for Frank had always believed in treating his mounts with gentleness, though he knew how to get the most out of them. Carrol was only now realizing how desperate Frank must have been on that ride, how much he must have hated hunting down his own brother: a shame and a duty in one courageous act.

The parson changed his saddle to the last horse on the banks of the Eagle River. He hadn't been saddle sore in years, but this wild ride had chafed layers of hide off his inner thighs and pounded his knees to aching mush. He mounted and rode in a long lope upstream. The horse had some gallop left in him, but Carrol decided to ride for distance instead of speed. He might get ten miles out of this horse at a lope.

As it turned out, he needed only six. He was following the wide trail trampled by the pilgrims, coming to the top of an incline, when he heard a voice and saw an armed man step into the path ahead of him.

"You stop!" the man demanded.

Carrol reined in the heaving mount and took a moment to size up the man in the trail. He appeared to an Indian, but wore the clothing of a white man, braids falling over his lapels. The preacher got down and gave his exhausted mount some slack in the saddle cinch. "Who are you, friend?" he said.

"Dan Feather. You?"

"I am the Reverend Carrol Moncrief. I'm looking for the Church of the Weeping Virgin."

Dan lowered his rifle. "Moncrief? Okay, you come on in." He motioned up the trail with his muzzle.

"Where is Dee Hassard?" the parson asked, leading his horse. Pain stabbed both knees after the hard ride, and walking felt awkward.

Dan Feather pointed his barrel upward. "Deacon Dee go up the mountain today. Go see cross. He take money."

"When did he leave?"

"Daylight."

Carrol nodded. Maybe there was time.

When they walked into the clearing, Carrol took a moment to judge what was going on. The place crawled like an ant bed, and the walls of a building at the top of the slope already stood four logs high. "What is this place?" he said.

"'Tigiwon," Dan Feather replied.

"What's that mean?"

"Sacred place."

A look of disbelief swept his face. This Dee Hassard sure had some line of gab to get these people here, building a town this high in the mountains. "Do me a favor, Dan Feather. Walk my horse a while. Rub him down. He's been used hard."

"I take good care," Dan promised and led the horse away on a level trail.

Carrol looked for someone who might be in charge, settling on a young man who was peeling logs with a good-looking woman. The pilgrims had begun to take notice of him by now, and some of them gravitated toward the log church to see what he wanted.

"Who are you?" James O'Rourke said, cordially, when the big man in black trudged up the slope to him.

He tipped his hat to the lady. "Name's Moncrief. Where's Hopewell? He hired me by correspondence to guide this party."

"He went with Deacon Hassard and two others up the mountain."

Carrol sighed. He was tired. "I need to borrow a horse or mule so I can catch 'em."

O'Rourke's brow wrinkled. "You can't ride where they've gone. Too rough. They'll be back this evening, though."

"I doubt it. Which way did they go?"

O'Rourke pointed. "What's the hurry all about?"

He studied their faces. The woman looked concerned. Maybe she had suspected something by now. But the youth beside her had been taken in.

"Dee Hassard is no more a deacon that this log is," he said, kicking the felled timber. "He's a swindler and a murderer. He shot my brother to death not long ago in South Park, and I mean to bring him down for it."

He watched carefully. The woman sank to the log and put her hands to her face, growing almost instantly pale. A body couldn't fake fear like that. The lad's face, on the other hand, remained blank for several long seconds, then grew angry, and finally turned to scowl at the woman.

"You're in it!" he said.

May gasped, thought quickly, realized how it must look to them. She glanced at the gathering crowd, saw their eyes piercing her.

"You joined the same time Hassard did!" O'Rourke said. "So did Clarence. You're all in it!"

"No!" May cried.

The pilgrims closed in on her.

"What about that man who came here yesterday? Supposed to be your husband? He was in it, too, and you three killed him to get a bigger cut, didn't you?"

"No!"

She stood up, and O'Rourke grabbed her by the arm as if she were trying to escape.

"Let her go!" Carrol ordered. "Get aholt of yourselves! This ain't no time to be makin' rash accusations. We'll sort this whole thing out after I get Hassard." He pushed his way past several pilgrims, starting up the slope.

"I'm comin' with you," May said. She was getting mad now. She had been first duped by Hassard, now wrongly accused by these pilgrims, and she was getting tired of it all. She might have taken it meekly before she met Clarence, but she was getting stronger for having known him.

"I'm goin' alone," Moncrief answered, without looking back.

"You just try to stop me," she insisted, her voice grating as even she had never heard. She knifed one of her accusers with a glare and hiked briskly in Moncrief's footsteps. "Clarence has a gun. He'll be in trouble if we don't hurry. We can follow the blaze marks on the trees."

Moncrief slowed his pace, and the woman stormed past him. Lord, give me strength, he thought. He was tired—so tired. And now, to go up this mountain on foot. Maybe the woman would help. He didn't blame her for not wanting to stay with the pilgrims. Also, she knew what had been going on with Hassard, so maybe she could fill him in. Anyway, he had no time to argue.

"Moncrief!" the youth cried.

The reverend swiveled his tired eyes.

"Yesterday Hassard rode up the valley on a big red mule, but he came back on foot. He said he fell off and the mule got away."

Carrol's eyes searched the young face and understood. Maybe Hassard had already established his escape route. Maybe it would be better to ride up the trail, find the mule, and wait for Hassard to come down to it. For some reason, he could only briefly consider it. Maybe it was because he was so tired of riding. The trail ahead was hot. Perhaps the cross was calling him up the mountain.

He took a few deep breaths and turned up the slope behind the woman. If this failed, Hassard was gone.

Twenty-eight

❧

They had climbed above the timberline for almost an hour now, and still the crest seemed a mile above them. Clarence was carrying the saddlebag full of money in addition to his own secret holdings in his jacket. Even with the extra weight, he stayed on Hassard's heels, and could have passed him if he had wanted. But Clarence preferred not to turn his back on Deacon Dee.

They came to the brink of a cliff that dropped untold hundreds of feet below them in a succession of narrow ledges scarcely fit for mountain goats. Clarence stopped for a moment and let Hassard trudge on up the trackless slope of cold rock and slick alpine tundra.

The view from the cliff spanned reaches that would require weeks of travel to fetch, and the Vermonter could not imagine why he had ever worried about the west filling up with people before he could get here. Across the many high peaks and forested valleys around him, he could see not one mark of settlement. Not a road, nor a field, nor a streak of smoke across the sky.

Hopewell came to his side and looked down the cliff, trying to gather in the sheer expanse of air below him, knowing now how the lowly world looked to the eagle.

"Did you ever think you'd see anything like this?" Clarence asked.

Hopewell shook his head reverently. "Didn't know there was such as this on all of God's whole earth."

"Let's throw a rock off," Clarence suggested, grinning at the elder.

Hopewell smiled boyishly, found a stone the size of a hen's egg. Clarence picked a like one, and they hurled them together as Mary Whitepath passed silently behind them. The stones arched unimpressively away from the precipice, then began plummeting downward, finally vanishing like flies into the sunlight. If they made a sound against something, it never reached the ears of those who had thrown them.

"Hey!" Hassard shouted from above. "Let's get goin' down there!"

Clarence saw a ridge above and climbed steadily toward it, containing his excitement. When he reached it, he found only a higher ridge beyond it. He knew they had to be near the divide, but here he was such a tiny speck on this vast mountain that he couldn't be sure which ridge was the highest.

He looked down toward Tigiwon but couldn't be certain where it lay anymore. The valley of the Eagle River—a long, straight furrow from the banks of the stream—had become invisible from here. It had shrunk away to a series of low dark places. The sun shone from on high now, and Clarence found bearings difficult to maintain in his mind. He was practically lost, turned so far around that he couldn't have hit Vermont with a rifle shot. Rationally, however, he knew that he must only continue upward to arrive at his destination. And they had left a trail of blaze marks and piles of stones to guide them back down the mountain.

He followed Hassard's lead, winding among countless snowfields and fans of huge boulders where peaks had crumbled in ancient times. The wind wanted his hat here, and he curled the brim hard to keep it on his head. Cool air rushed in and out of his lungs, fueling him well even with its dearth of oxygen.

It seemed they were climbing to the top of the world, and Clarence looked up only occasionally now, between steps. Always the mountain loomed ahead of him, like a planet whose curve he could never traverse. But suddenly, rounding a small peak of huge stone rubble, he saw the entire sky open below and ahead of him where the mountain had lain before. Here the world fell away in every direction except for the ridge winding away to his right, which he suddenly knew was the summit of Notch Mountain. And here was its divide under his feet.

Hassard was standing ahead of him. Just standing, for the first time today, taking in some view. Clarence came further around the small peak, and then saw it. Like a far-away painting whose canvas trailed off into infinity. It seemed almost touchable, yet between its face and the Vermonter's eyes lay a void no cannon shot could span.

The paragon of mountain peaks rose high across a basin like a near-perfect pyramid of rock. Upon its face, in gossamer lines of pure white snow, the cross stabbed Clarence's eyes as a beautiful blaring trumpet might assault his ears. Its arms lifted upward like a conductor holding an orchestra at perpetual readiness. Far friendlier than any beams of square-hewn timber, the snowy lines of the cross reclined comfortably against the cold granite. And though they may have stood wide as a town square, from here the lines were mere brush strokes of snow driven into unbelievable crevices.

"That's God's own easel," Hassard said.

The voice startled Clarence, and he realized that he had let the deacon circle behind him. He turned quickly to look, but found Hassard sitting harmlessly on a rock in the cold sunshine.

It was not as if the thought hadn't occurred to Dee Hassard, too. His pistol was easily reachable inside his coat. He had made sure of that. Neither Hopewell nor the Indian woman carried a weapon. It would have been a simple matter to put a bullet through the Vermonter's back, chase the elder and Mary Whitepath back down the mountain, and then angle southward to find his mule. Hell, he might have left all three of them dead on this mountain and let that cross of snow serve as their ridiculous headstone. He was already on the run for killing Frank Moncrief. What would another body or two matter?

But Dee Hassard had his pride. A killing to him was messy. It showed a lack of professionalism. He was more meticulous than that. Besides, he liked letting them live, letting them know how badly he had fooled them. That was part of the game. No, that *was* the game. Often he had wished he could be there when the realization struck—to see the looks of anger, shame, and panic meld suddenly on their faces. Murder was sometimes necessary—take Frank Moncrief and Charlie Holt. No way around either one of them.

But not here. This was too perfect. Look at their mouths hanging open. Look at them gawking across this basin at that crooked snow formation. It was laughable, and in days to come, Dee Hassard would laugh hard over it. There was still a chance that he could pull this thing off without killing Clarence. He hoped they would all live long to think about this one.

"It's just like the Weeping Virgin told me in my dreams. Let your burden down, Brother Clarence. It belongs to God now." In a way, he actually meant it. Dee Hassard was his own god, and these mortals were sacrificing to him now and didn't even know it.

Clarence looked at Hopewell, but the elder's eyes were across the basin. To leave this money here was foolish-

ness. But was it really his concern? They had allowed
Hassard to leave this morning with the church coffers.
They had prayed for him. It was their money—church
money. The congregation had to decide what to do with
it, ridiculous or not.

Oh well, he thought, letting the saddlebags slide off his
broad shoulder, at least I won't have to carry it back
down the mountain. He studied Hassard. The man was
staring just as long and reverently at the Snowy Cross as
Elder Hopewell or Mary Whitepath. Yet the Vermonter
knew it was far from over. An unnamed tension stood
between him and the deacon like a magnetic field:
opposing poles pushing against each other. You must
not turn your back on this man. He is not what he claims.
He will return for this money, and then it will be your
concern.

Mary Whitepath was on her knees, weeping silently,
staring at the cross.

The others sat in silence for several long minutes, and
Hassard paced through the logistics one more time.
Tonight, after a couple of hours of sleep, he would sneak
away from Tigiwon. Slipping past Clarence would be the
hardest part, but he would have an excuse planned in case
the Vermonter questioned him, and the dagger in his
pocket in the event the excuse failed to satisfy. Back in
the cities, he had learned how to stick a man so that he
would not even cry out. He would only die.

Next he would climb back up here to retrieve his earnings, a half-moon to light his way. Had any man in his
profession ever pulled off such a feat? By dawn he would
be mounting his mule and riding up the valley, about the
same time Carrol Moncrief arrived at Tigiwon. It would
be grueling, but after Buena Vista, he could sleep in the
stagecoach on his way to California.

He repeated each step in his mind until he began to feel
the chill of his own sweat. "Well, let's get back to
Tigiwon," he said, springing to his feet.

Clarence let the surprise show on his face. "Already?"

Hassard shrugged. "It's a long walk. We'd better get back before dark. The others will be waiting to hear about this." He started down the barren ridge without once looking back. "It's not as if we can't come back whenever we want to."

Clarence looked at the leather pouches stuffed with gold and currency and nodded. Yes, he thought. And Dee Hassard will want to come back tonight.

The snowfields had become so numerous around them that there was no other way. Going around them would mean retracing hundreds of feet back down the mountain, and neither Petra nor Ramon cared to lose any altitude at this point. Their path lay upward.

They had crossed some narrow streaks of snow already, but the one now in their path stretched almost a hundred yards and covered an old rock slide. Petra went first, wading into the field of white, crunching through its dirty surface.

"Be sure to feel for every step," Ramon warned. "You might fall into a hole or something."

"Yes," she said. "I will be careful."

After several steps, they sank waist deep into the drift, and snow was falling into the tops of Ramon's short boots, packing hard around his ankles. He said nothing of it, only wanting to reach the other side.

He paused to look around him. He had seen many new things on this journey, but this was something he had to remember. Here it seemed that some blight had lain waste to the whole warm world of trees and grass. Everything he saw was rock and snow, from the slick boulder under his heels to the distant ranges a hundred miles away. If there was still greenery below, he would never have known it from this vantage.

Coming finally out of the snowfield, Petra stomped the ice crystals from her legs and Ramon sat down to dump the packed snow from his boots. The nun happened to look at a chunk of ice Ramon cast aside and saw a crimson hue to it. "Are you bleeding?" she said.

The boy shrugged. "The snow packed in my boot and scraped me a little. It's nothing." He stood and looked up the slope. They seemed very near the top of the divide, but he had thought that many times today. "Let's look over this ridge."

He started slowly, letting Petra pull ahead of him. He almost dreaded peering over the crest. What if they found another, higher ridge a mile away? How long could they keep going? They could not get caught here by darkness. Soon they would have to go below.

What was he doing here, anyway? The reason was so old and far away that he almost couldn't bring it to mind. The Snowy Cross—that was it. Why? To save Guajolote. How? How was any of this going to help? Does gold lie scattered atop this range in the thousands of dollars?

"Ramon?"

He looked up and saw Petra standing straight and rigid on the crest above eye level. A fresh wind was trailing her hair behind her, and she looked like some kind of conquering princess. She didn't look down at him, but her hand waved for him to join her.

Already his heart was pounding, for he knew what he would find when he scrambled up the last of the incline. Then his heart stopped as the vision struck him. It was like brilliant light shining through a cross-carved door into a darkened room. He felt Petra's arms around him, his own around her, as a power surged between them whose force was greater than the sum of anything they could have mustered apart. Then she sank to her knees, and Ramon was left alone.

For a long moment he stared at the Mount of the Snowy Cross, marveling at his arrival here. Then, suddenly, he thought of home. Guajolote, where warm adobe soaked in sunlight and spring water laughed from miniature cascades. And for a moment, he felt a glimmer of faith strong enough to cause him to look around—around his feet first, as if he would find gold coin stacked there waiting for him. His eyes pulled to the right, following the ridge that rose to the summit of Notch Mountain. There was rough rock and patches of coarse snow—and something that glowed with the luster of time-smoothed leather.

He blinked hard and looked again at the object standing not fifty yards away on the ridge. A pair of leather saddlebags perched on the crest as if some hand had just deposited them there. He thought about the American photographer, Señor Jackson, whom he and Petra had met in Del Norte. The photographic party must have left this thing behind.

He left Petra and climbed an easy slope to the saddle-bags. Stooping, he lifted the bags, finding them heavier than he had imagined. He dropped them and heard a chink of metal. What he was thinking wasn't possible, of course, but it made his stomach flutter nonetheless. He glanced at the Snowy Cross, looming across the high basin through a cloud-haze that was beginning to form. He looked at Petra, the quintessence of devotion there on her knees in this unlikely place. Was her faith alone sufficient?

He knelt and unfastened the buckle on one of the pouches. Slowly he lifted the flap and peered inside. For a splinter of a moment he knew what it felt like to have been brushed by the wake of angels passing nearby. He tried to call Petra's name, but couldn't speak. Ramon del Bosque was never again to know the careless indifference of boyhood.

Twenty-nine

❧

They came to the place where Clarence and Elder Hopewell had thrown the stones into the void, and they paused there to look again across the uninviting mountainscape. They could see the dark forest from here, and Clarence longed to be back in its shadow, back where tall things grew. But it was impossible to pass this place without stopping to look over.

Hopewell and Mary Whitepath stood to his left, Hassard slightly downhill to his right, anxious to move on. Then Clarence saw Mary Whitepath's arm raise toward him, her finger pointing back down the trail toward Tigiwon. Clarence looked, and he saw climbers just above the timberline.

"By golly, that's May," he said, astonished. "Who the devil is that with her?"

Dee Hassard took one look and felt panic whir in his

brain. How could that be Carrol Moncrief? He had underestimated the big circuit rider, but that didn't matter now.

Clarence saw Hassard begin to turn. He thought about Charlie Holt's pistol, strapped now around his hips under his jacket. He tried to get at it, but the jacket was buttoned. Hassard had come around to face him now, a hand inside his coat. Clarence tried to lift the bottom of his jacket over the gun grip, but the gold coins stacked on edge in the fabric slowed the attempt. It was too late now, anyway. He was looking down the barrel of Hassard's Colt. He saw the orange flare and the smoke, but he never heard the report, never felt the slug.

Hassard watched, satisfied to see the Vermonter fly backward over the cliff. He trained his muzzle on Hopewell, then Mary Whitepath. No need. Neither could harm him.

"Don't follow!" he shouted, glaring wildly into their stares of horror and astonishment.

Dee Hassard shoved the Colt back into Frank Moncrief's holster and sprinted up the mountain. It was a footrace now, and one that he could not afford to lose.

It seemed to take him only a few minutes to reach the divide, but when he got there, his lungs were ready to rip. He scrambled around the peak of rubble and slid to a standstill, almost swallowing his tongue in his surprise. A small, pretty, dark-haired woman and a black-haired boy were hunkered over the money, counting, calculating. Pilgrims? No, he didn't recognize them from the congregation. What in the name of . . .

Dee Hassard fought for oxygen as he glanced back down toward Moncrief. He drew his Colt, the boy and the woman shrinking away from its muzzle. "Put it back in the bags!" he managed.

Sister Petra felt a calm come over her. The Snowy Cross was out of her sight over her left shoulder, but she felt its solid presence. She obeyed the stranger, methodically placing the cold specie, the paper notes, and the pouches of gold dust back into the saddlebag openings.

"Who the hell are you?" Hassard demanded, annoyed. Maybe it was a good thing he had been driven back up here, or these thieves would have gotten his earnings.

"I am Petra, and this is Ramon."

Hassard snorted and shook his head. This was too much to take in, and he really didn't care. The woman had finished replacing the money, and now she stood with the saddlebags draped over her right forearm. She stepped in front of the boy.

"Give them to me!" Hassard ordered.

"I cannot," she said. "This does not belong to you." It was so clear and simple that she didn't have to think about it. It was so obviously right that she didn't have to fear.

Hassard felt Moncrief too close behind. There was no time for this. He reached for the bag, grabbed a leather strap. The woman would not turn it loose. She possessed some grip, and Dee Hassard was tired. Could he wrestle her? What about that Mexican boy? Mexicans carried knives, didn't they?

Ramon had stepped to Petra's right, trying to see some sense in all this. What were they saying in that damned numb-tongued English? He was afraid of this orange-haired stranger, but Petra seemed perfectly at ease holding on to her prayers answered. He was about to tell her to let the stranger have the money when the gun fired and Petra crumpled backward onto the sharp rocks. The muzzle swung toward him, but he ignored it, falling on top of the good sister.

Hassard panted hard. The boy was no threat. He had to run now. Moncrief was too close behind him. He threw the winnings over his shoulder and smiled as he angled southward down the slope. Damn, what a couple of close ones!

Arriving at the bluff with May, Carrol found Elder Hopewell and Mary Whitepath lying on their stomachs, looking over the precipice.

"Don't move!" the gangling black man was shouting. "Clarence. Don't move!"

May screamed and threw herself between them, looking over the edge. She saw Clarence lying on his back some thirty feet below, his chest heaving. He rested on a narrow gravelly ledge that sloped dangerously downward. One arm and one leg hung over the edge. Below lay a series of ledges, each too slim to stand upon. If the Vermonter slid one inch, he would fall hundreds of feet, bouncing off hard rock ledges all the way down.

Carrol gritted his teeth as he looked over the edge. From below, he had looked up just in time to see the tall young man take Hassard's bullet in the chest. It was amazing that he had survived at all, but now he was almost surely doomed. Either he would have to climb back up to the ledge, or someone would have to climb down to put a rope on him. The young man's chances were slim, but Carrol did not feel good about leaving these two women and this old man to handle it.

Then he heard the shot—a single pistol blast from above. "Are there more of you up there?" he asked the black man.

"No," Hopewell said.

May had sprung from the rocks to fetch the coil of rope Hopewell had thrown from his shoulders.

Carrol made a hard decision. His job was to get Hassard, bring him to justice for killing Frank. Bring him in or kill him. He was getting mad. May had told him about the death of Charlie Holt, and he had just seen Hassard shoot this young man in cold blood with his own eyes. The con man had turned murderer and left a virtual trail of dead bodies all over Colorado. These three would have to handle the young man on the ledge. He turned and sprinted up the mountain.

Coming to the divide, Carrol drew his pistol and came around a cone of timeworn boulders. He heard a scuffle of feet on the rock and found it quickly. The boy looked at him with tear-filled eyes. In his arms was a woman whose blood stained the front of her frock in a hue of crimson bright as a cardinal. Her eyes were blinking, but her body lay limp. Trying to lift her, the boy caught sight of Carrol and gasped.

Quickly the parson put his revolver in the holster and came toward the unlikely pair. "Put her down," he said.

The boy replied in Spanish: "Help me. She wants to look at the cross."

"La cruz?" Carrol said, picking out the few words he recognized. He let his eyes focus for the first time on the distant mountain slope across the basin, and saw the lines of snow driven there. He put his arms under the woman, a slight creature whose green eyes glistened serenely at him. With help from the boy, he lifted her, turned her, carried her to the very brink of the divide and made her as comfortable as possible on the rocks.

Looking southward down the slope, Carrol thought of Hassard slipping away. If he reached the red mule he had left up the valley, he would likely go free. He sprang to his feet and ran a few yards along the divide. He could see no sign of the murderer. Trailing him would be slow, while Hassard would be running like a mountain goat, widening the gap between them.

He could think of just one way. Return to that town those lunatic pilgrims were building, borrow a mount, and try to ride Hassard down somewhere on the trail.

When he came back to the dying woman, the boy with her had dried his eyes and was listening to her. Carrol understood little, for she spoke only Spanish, though she didn't look Mexican—not with those green eyes.

"My life has been a glory," Petra was saying, holding Ramon's hand, glancing away from the cross to him. "But I will not leave this place. Now it is up to you. You must save Guajolote."

"But, Sister," Ramon said. "The money is gone. That man took it away."

She smiled. "Have faith. The Lord will provide. You must not go home until you know how to save your village."

Thirty

❧

He could hear May's voice echoing across the mountains somewhere, far away. "Grab the rope!" she was saying.

Clarence tried to make sense of it. His chest felt as if someone had driven a wagon over it. Sharp things poked him in the rear end. An arm and a leg dangled off something, feeling cold, and he was gasping for breath.

"Damn you, Clarence Philbrick! You grab ahold of that rope!"

What was she talking about? There was something flopping around on his stomach. It felt like a snake, but he knew somehow not to move. Slowly he opened his eyes and saw the rock rising above him to his right, felt the emptiness to his left. The rope was undulating above him. There was May's face, looking angrily down at him. Sister Mary Whitepath and Elder Hopewell were there beside her.

Now he remembered the loud blast from Hassard's pistol and gathered where he was. His chest hurt like hell, but he felt no blood warmth, no bleeding inside. The coins, lined in pairs up and down his jacket must have saved him. He had always heard stories like that—men surviving shoot-outs and pistol duels when bullets glanced off coins or whiskey flasks or pocket watches.

"Clarence!" May repeated. "Grab the rope. You're about to slide off!"

Sure enough, the Vermonter could feel his body pulling away from the face of the cliff, wanting to roll on the gravel. He raised his right hand slowly and put it on the rope, taking a wrap. But he couldn't imagine even sitting up right now, much less climbing twenty feet of line.

"Good," May said, though she hardly sounded as if she approved. "Now, you've got to tie yourself on."

Suddenly he felt himself slide and found an instant store of strength. His cold left hand swung to the rope and pain like a knife wound tore into his chest. He slid over the little ledge he was on, and May screamed like nothing he had ever heard. He hit the end of the rope, the wrap he had taken twisting hard around his right hand, clamping down on it like a vise.

Short of breath, Clarence kicked his feet, searching for a foothold, finding none. His strength was almost sapped, his chest racked in one great excruciating throb. He was going to have to pull himself up, hand over hand. He had done it before. Rope-climbing had been part of his exercise routine back home. But never while wearing twenty-five extra pounds of gold. Never while suffering an impact to the chest like a mule's kick.

"Pull yourself up, Clarence!" May was near hysteria. "Pull yourself back up to the ledge, damn it!"

He couldn't imagine her cussing like that. He pulled up with both arms, the rope feeling as if it would pinch his right hand in two. He didn't have the strength to raise himself more than an inch. He was going to have to do something quick. He was growing weaker by the breath, and breath was short.

It was the gold! Damn his father's gold! It had weighed on him his life long, and now it was killing him, literally, as it had slowly suffocated him since he was a boy.

It was time to shed the burden, if it wasn't too late. Clarence released his left hand, letting his whole weight hang from the right hand with the rope wrapped around it. May yodeled in terror, thinking he had lost his grip, and the pain from the rope twisting his right hand made a tear cloud Clarence's eye. Clumsily, fighting the searing agony in his chest, he flopped his left arm until the heavy sleeve slid off.

He paused, for the next move seemed impossible. He had to take the rope in his left hand, release his right, and let the death jacket fall. How could he hold on with his left hand, with the pain concentrated in the left side of his chest? Feeling weaker, he knew he must act. The pain of the rope crushing his right hand was unbearable, anyway. Death on the rocks below could not possibly be more painful.

A sore ache and a knife-edged pang collided in the Vermonter's chest as he took hold of the rope with his left hand. The twist snapped away from his right hand, and the rope burned his left palm as it plowed past all the grip he could muster.

"Clarence!" May screamed, her voice a demanding censure.

Quickly he let his right arm drop and felt the sleeve slip over his wrist. He looked down to see the oilskin jacket snag but a short distance below on a sharp rock that might have broken his back had he fallen on it. He saw the bullet hole near the left lapel, a singular glint of gold metal glowing from it.

With his right hand on the hemp again, Clarence achieved enough purchase to stop slipping down the rope. But now what? Dropping the gold had helped, but he couldn't hang here long. He still couldn't pull himself up, exhausted as he was, weakened by the blow to the chest.

Now something crept into the Vermonter's mind. He had learned a few basic mountaineering skills from a college friend who liked to scale rocky places in the White Mountains. There was a way to hang here almost effortlessly, and a way to move across the face of this cliff to safer ground.

He felt the rope against his left knee, ran it first between his legs, then under his left thigh. Taking the dangling end of the rope in his left hand, he ran it across his chest, lifted it over his head, and let it fall over his right shoulder. Now he took a firm grip with his left hand on the loose end of the rope hanging down his back.

Clarence felt the familiar bite of the rope under his thigh and over his shoulder. *Abseil.* That was the name of this maneuver. Used in descending steep grades. The friction of the rope running under his thigh and over his shoulder took a share of his weight, easing the task on his hands. His palms served only as brakes now, to keep the rope from slipping around his body.

"Good!" May was saying. "You're thinking now."

He turned his eyes upward, feeling lighter, stronger, free of his father's weight, his father's intimidating success. He spoke something silently to himself that was stronger than a vow. He would be independent from here to death. He would rely on his own energies, his own abilities. His father's wealth could sink to the pits of hell for all he cared. Clarence Philbrick was his own man.

"Do something!" May shouted. "You can't just hang there!" She didn't see how he had managed this much. Hadn't a bullet bowled him off this ledge?

She was right, Clarence thought. Now, before his last stores of energy failed him. He looked to both sides, found a place to the left and below him where he could stand. From there, his eyes found a series of crags and ledges that would give him toeholds, handholds, all the way up to the brink where May and the others could pull him to safety.

He hadn't done it in a few years, but the method reeled from his trained muscles like second nature. He let himself slip cautiously downward, the rope smarting where it cut under his thigh and over the opposite shoulder. Now he remembered the drawback of the abseil method. It hurt! Here the cliff face sloped outward, and he managed to get his feet situated squarely on it. His legs pressing against the rock took still more weight, and the grip required of his hands lessened.

Still, he had to remember. His grip was the only thing that kept him from falling hundreds of feet. The wind was cool around him in this strange place, so high and wild. Sweat braced his brow. He looked below, saw the jacket just ten feet under him, his own rope lying over it. He disregarded it. It was the last thing he needed.

"What are you doing?" May said, for he had slipped beyond her sight over the ledges.

Good question, he thought. Why put it off longer? He took a few steps to his left along the cliff face, then swung like a pendulum back to center and beyond. He repeated the maneuver, each time swinging farther, until he was able to drop onto the flat ledge he had spotted from above.

The relief was instant. Pain ebbed from his palms, his shoulder, the underpart of his thigh. Only the left side of his chest still smarted, and even that had loosened up with the exercise.

Tying the rope around his waist as a safety line, Clarence began climbing up the series of handgrips and footholds he had located before. May scrambled along the cliff face to meet him, Mary Whitepath and Elder Hopewell close behind her.

When he got near the ledge, they reached down to grab his shirt and raised him up. They dragged him onto the rock, and May fell on him crying, searching him for wounds, finding only a little blood caused by the fall.

"It's a miracle," Hopewell said. "The shot hit him in the chest. I saw his left shoulder jerk back when Hassard fired." With his long fingers, he probed the area where the bullet should have hit.

May was sobbing on top of him now, feeling warm. "It's a miracle, all right," Clarence managed to say, though every word hurt.

Clarence was on his feet when the two strangers came down from the divide. One was a tall man in a dusty black suit. He wore a revolver that had seen much service, and a visage of utter fatigue and failure mixed on his face.

The boy was sad and quiet and looked as if his faculties were not all with him. He looked like Clarence felt, and Clarence wanted to know what had happened.

"Let's get down to the timber first," Moncrief said, "and make a camp for you folks before dark. Then we'll sort this out."

They built a fire in the timber, divvied a meager supply of jerked venison. Elder Hopewell began, telling Moncrief about the Church of the Weeping Virgin, from the first days.

"What now?" the reverend asked, after he had heard the fantastic story.

Hopewell shook his head and looked sadly into the fire, drained, exhausted. "Its over for me. Something went wrong, and I don't even know when or where. We're not a church anymore. We're lost. I knew that when I saw the Snowy Cross. That cross has been there thousands of years, I guess. It will last. The Church of the Weeping Virgin won't."

The boy's story was the hardest to get clear. He seemed dazed, unwilling to speak. But Mary Whitepath was Comanche, and knew Spanish better than she knew English. At length, she got the boy started, and it became a glory for Ramon to recount his journey with Sister Petra.

May noticed a peculiar look on Clarence's face when the boy mentioned the village of Guajolote and the Ojo de los Brazos land grant that Sister Petra had sought to save. The more she watched him, the more astounded he seemed, and she hoped the fall hadn't rattled something in his head.

"He says they came into this valley south of here," Mary Whitepath interpreted, "and they found a big red mule with hobbles on, so they camped there."

Moncrief's interest peaked. He squinted his eyes and turned one ear to May. "Didn't Hassard claim a big red mule threw him somewhere up the trail?"

"Yes, but if that's true, what would the mule be doing wearing hobbles?"

Mary Whitepath broke in: "The boy says an old man came to get the mule, and this old man told him and the sister where to find the cross on the mountain. Then the old man took the mule away."

"Ask him what the old man's name was," Moncrief ordered.

"He does not know the name, but he says it was the old man the people talked about in Buena Vista. The one who got lost and found the cross so high on the mountain."

"Sounds like the same old prospector we saw down at Tigiwon," Clarence added. "Didn't get his name. Hassard was the only one who talked to him."

"Did he have a mule with him then?" Moncrief said.

"No," the Vermonter said. "He carried a pack on his back."

Carrol grinned at the ground. It sounded for all the world as if old Jules Billings had come to take Hassard's big red mule away. Jules was in the ground on the banks of the Blue River, but it was a happy thought, however impossible. No telling how many played-out prospectors there were tramping around in these hills, looking for another 'forty-nine.

Ramon tugged Mary Whitepath's sleeve, for he wasn't

through. "We did everything we were supposed to do," he told her. "We found the cross. We even found the money to save the village. And then that man came and shot Sister Petra and took the money away from us." He covered his face with a hand. "I couldn't do anything. The man had a gun, and it happened before I could do anything."

They sat in silence after Mary Whitepath translated for them.

"Tell him to keep the faith," Clarence said suddenly to the translator. Then he looked right at the boy. "Your Sister Petra would want you to keep the faith, boy. If you do, I guarantee you'll get the money you need to carry out what she wanted."

"I wouldn't make promises I can't keep," Moncrief warned. "Even if I manage to catch up to Hassard, all the money he's got belongs to other people."

Clarence shot a sure glance at him. "I can keep my promises, Reverend. Sister Mary, tell that boy he'll have the money he needs."

The parson's brow wrinkled, but he didn't have time for argument. "I'm goin' back down to the big camp," he said, rising. "Maybe there's a chance that old miner you all ran into took Hassard's red mule up the valley." He chuckled. "The Lord works in ways like that sometimes. You never know. Maybe I can catch up to him."

"You can take my horse when you get to Tigiwon," Clarence said.

Carrol dipped his hat brim. "Obliged. Walk with me a little ways down the trail," he said. "I want to talk to you."

Clarence rose and followed the big reverend out of camp.

"Tell that Mexican boy to stay with the pilgrims," Moncrief ordered. "After I get Hassard, I'll come back for him and take him to his village in New Mexico."

Clarence nodded.

Moncrief reached into the breast pocket of his coat and

pulled out the certificate Edgar Dreyer had given him in Frisco. "You'll take this in payment for your horse. Don't argue with me, because I don't even know that it's worth the paper it's printed on."

"What is it?" Clarence asked, unfolding the certificate.

"Mining claim over near Frisco. I got it in payment for a funeral I preached there. I've got no use for it. I ain't no miner."

Clarence nodded and tucked the claim into his pants pocket.

"One other thing," Moncrief said. "I ought to know better than to stick my nose into another man's business, but if you don't marry that girl over there, you're a blasted idiot. God intended some couples to pair off, and if they can't see it, well, somebody ought to have sense enough to tell 'em. I'm duly vested by the Territory of Colorado to perform the rites of matrimony, and if Dee Hassard doesn't sneak a bullet through my skull, I'd consider it an honor to conduct the ceremony myself."

Clarence bristled a little at first, for he was his own man, but he saw Carrol Moncrief's intentions for good ones and nodded with a smile on his face. "Good luck," he said, shaking the big man's hand.

It was like a dream that May would remember at odd moments as long as she lived, and it would move her more each time she thought of it.

She woke in the night when she sensed some movement in camp and found Clarence adding wood to the fire. He smiled at her to let her know everything was all right. Later she woke again; the fire was flickering nicely, but Clarence was gone. She slept quite a while before waking a third time, and found him kneeling at the fire again, probing it with a stick. She was curious now, so she sat up, but he cautioned her with his open palm and held a finger to his lips, glancing at the boy, Ramon, who slept nearby.

In the morning Clarence woke them and told Ramon to

stoke the fire. As the boy went to gather wood, May found the coil of rope on the ground near Clarence's bedroll. She was sure she had left that rope trailing over the ledge yesterday after rescuing Clarence. When she questioned him with a look, he answered her with a wry smile—a smile that would lodge in her mind's eye and mean more to her every day.

It was only a few minutes later that Ramon was on his hands and knees, fanning the embers of the fire with his hat. He was feeling lonely, mourning Petra, missing Guajolote. The Indian woman had gone off into the woods somewhere, so he didn't even have anybody to talk to.

Then the ashes flew away from something, and Ramon cried out.

Thirty-one

❖

Carrol was no expert tracker, but he knew enough to read the desperation in Dee Hassard's trail. He had found the camp at daylight—seen the nun's diminutive tracks, the boy's, the large curve of the big red mule's.

The old miner who had taken the mule left no tracks at all. Maybe he wore moccasins, Carrol thought. Maybe he had learned some Indian trick. Maybe. It didn't matter. He had to keep his mind focused on Hassard.

The swindler's tracks had come down from Notch Mountain and were falling on top of the mule's prints now. The trail was easy enough to read from the back of Clarence Philbrick's horse. Hassard had made no attempt to cover his trail. He was in too much of a hurry. He was short, the parson recalled. Maybe five-foot-seven. But this was the stride of a six-footer. Dee Hassard had been running for his life when he left these prints, trying to catch that mule.

But by now he had to know it was too late. The mule had headed into a small creek valley whose slopes had grown steeper, evolving gradually into a box canyon. Hassard was trapped here. Even if he managed to catch the mule, his only way out would be back down the mouth of the canyon.

Carrol passed over a spot where Hassard had stopped to rest. He made out the place where the heavy bag of gold and money had plastered a cool patch of green grass to the ground. He let his mount's head bob three times, then pulled up, looking back at the place.

He had caught an inkling of something. Hassard never stopped to rest. He had stopped here to think. He had known by this time that he would not get away clean. He had stopped to plan something, like the gun he had planted at the South Platte camp to kill Frank.

It would be something different for Carrol, of course. Ambush? Probably not. Carrol would be expecting that. He knew how to move into a possible ambush, keeping to cover. He had learned that in his old rustling days, when the vigilantes had marked him for execution. He would be able to read an ambush here. Besides, Hassard was more of a back shooter than a sharp-shooter.

It would be trickier than a mere ambush. That was Hassard's style. His guile beat all. He had thought way ahead of Frank, and Frank had been the most thorough of lawmen. It was going to be something unexpected.

While Carrol was trying to guess ahead, Dee Hassard suddenly came walking into view with his hands in the air. The preacher turned the horse, drew his revolver.

"Easy, Moncrief," the redhead cried, stopping in his tracks. "I'm givin' up. You've got me cornered. I'd rather take my chances with the hangman later than have you shoot me in this godforsaken place."

Carrol rode forward, his sights trained on the murderer. His jaw muscles tensed so hard they hurt. He noticed

Hassard's empty holster. Tricky bastard thinks I won't shoot him unarmed. He came within a few paces of the swindler and swung down from the horse. "Where's your gun?" he said.

"I lost it," Hassard said.

Carrol smirked.

"I wouldn't believe it if I was you either, but it's true. Anyway, you can see I don't have it on me." He turned around with his hands in the air.

Carrol knew he was lying. May Tremaine had told him that Hassard carried two pistols. How could a man lose two? The funny thing was that he knew Hassard didn't expect him to believe the story. Dealing with this swindler was like wresting with a man's mind. Well, there was only one thing to do. Teach Hassard a new hold. Do something unexpected. Throw him off guard.

There was a rope tied to Carrol's saddle. "So, you'd rather face the hangman?" He took the rope down and tossed it to Hassard. "Build yourself a loop."

"You're not gonna hang me. That's murder, Moncrief."

"What jury would convict me for hangin' a nun killer?"

"Nun?" Hassard said, as if insulted. "What nun?"

"Sister Petra of the Snowy Cross. You killed her yesterday up on the divide."

"I didn't know she was a nun! What in the hell would a nun be doin' a way out here?"

Carrol shook his head. "Just put the noose on. I'd as soon shoot you if you don't."

"You're forgettin' something," Hassard said. "The money!"

"I don't give a damn about the money."

"I hid it good," Hassard said. "You won't find it without me."

"I said I don't give a damn about the money. I just want to free the world of your stench, and the quicker the better."

"But there's thousands!" Hassard cried, dropping to his

knees. "Please, let me take you to it! Let me live just that much longer!" Real tears poured from his eyes.

Carrol laughed. "All right, you can get up now, that's all I wanted to know."

Hassard stared.

"Well, get up! You didn't really think I'd lynch you, did you? You didn't really think you could fool me with all that whimperin' after what you pulled on me in Denver, did you?"

Hassard sniffed and got to his feet. A cold pit began to form in his stomach. Yes, he had thought Moncrief really was going to lynch him. He had been taken in. He couldn't believe he had fallen for that part about the nun. He had lost the edge, and he knew it. Worse yet, he knew Moncrief knew it.

"Show me where the money is," Moncrief ordered. "But don't go grabbin' at it real quick, because I know what you'll pull out." He grinned and twisted his revolver in the air.

Reluctantly, Hassard turned back up the canyon, his hands above his head. Carrol followed, anxiously watching every move. He couldn't help remembering how Frank had let his guard down. How he himself had been so readily taken in that night in Denver. Was Dee Hassard ever finished conniving?

They came into a grove of aspens—a pleasant place within earshot of running water, with summer-green leaves filtering the sun onto the white tree trunks. It was an older grove with bigger trees, well spaced. The two men wound their way among the trees, and Hassard rested his palms on top of his hat, for the lowest limbs swept just over his head, and his arms were tired.

"It's there," Hassard said, thrusting his chin toward a hollow log. It had been a large pine tree, long dead now, still showing vestiges of charcoal from some prehistoric forest fire. Aspens grew up on both sides of it like andirons holding it in place.

Carrol was taking no chances. He kept thinking about

what Clarence Philbrick and May Tremaine had told him. Hassard had waited until the last moment to kill Charlie Holt. He trusted no move the little man made. He wasn't even willing to reach into the hollow log for the saddlebags. Maybe that was what Hassard wanted. A trap of some kind in there? Something to break his arm? Maybe Hassard was still thinking ahead of him.

Putting his muzzle against the back of Hassard's neck, he said, "Reach in there real slow. One hand. Any move you make too quick will get you killed."

Hassard trembled, and it was with real fear now. Moncrief had him as turned around as old Jules Billings before he found the Snowy Cross. He had never had a game turn this bad on him, and it made his senses swim. What Moncrief would do with him next was a terror and a mystery. Maybe the big preacher really would hang him. Maybe that woman on the mountain really was a nun. He couldn't say. He didn't know. He just reached into the log slowly, slipped his palm carefully under the leather, and drew the saddlebags out.

"Put it down and back away over yonder," Carrol ordered. He kept his sights trained on the vest buttons as the little sneak shrank away in small, timid steps.

"Don't kill me," Hassard blurted. "For the love of God, Moncrief, don't kill me here." Tears burst from his eyes like a flood.

"Shut your trap," the preacher growled, disgusted. He looked down at the saddlebags and turned back the flap of the near pouch. Inside he found the .36-caliber Smith & Wesson, rust pitted, cocked, lying on top of a stack of paper money.

Frank's Colt must be in the other pouch, he thought. Or . . .

Frank had gotten him almost to Cañon City. Almost to the penitentiary. He had let his guard down.

The thought shot at him like a lightning bolt, and from the corner of his eye, he saw that Hassard was still backing away, timidly, in little shuffling steps. Even before his eyes could glance up, the notion was in his head, and he remembered a low limb behind the crown of Hassard's hat. Backing toward it now, his hands in the air, pleading, blubbering, conniving.

Carrol's eyes came up, wild and alert, and saw Hassard's desperation. It was already happening. Dee Hassard was pretending to trip backward over a rotten limb in the grass. His hands were reaching for the low-hanging limb above him, as if to catch himself from the fall. Frank's pistol was up there. Lodged in a fork or something. It wasn't in the saddlebags at all. Hassard was one beat ahead, and there was no time to think.

Carrol let the barrel find its mark, tightened his grip on the trigger. He saw the murdering little swindler hump in midair, the blast whipping him to the ground as the rotten limb in the grass caught his heel.

The parson sprang, cocked the revolver for another shot. He looked down at Hassard and found the pale blue eyes open, reflecting flickers of light on fluttering aspen leaves. He kicked him once or twice, just to be sure. He checked for warm breath, pausing long.

Finally, Carrol Moncrief let the hammer spring rest on his revolver and slipped the weapon back into its holster. He sighed, trying to exhale the ball of nausea in his gut.

He looked now at the tree limb above the dead man, but found no revolver there. No knife. Nothing.

Stepping slowly to the saddlebags, he knelt, and shot yet another reassuring glance at the body. He opened the leather flap of the second pouch and found Frank's .45-caliber Colt inside, cocked, resting on a pouch of gold dust.

Dee Hassard had finally connived himself to death.

Thirty-two

❧

In years to come, Ramon would tell it often to the children of Guajolote: how the gold Sister Petra had prayed for appeared in the coals of that high mountain campfire in the country of the Snowy Cross. And the children's parents and grandparents would tell them it was true, for they had been there the day Ramon returned to Guajolote with the gold coins, back when he was just a boy.

"Why Guajolote?" the incredulous young ones would ask, crowding around the good father in the shade of a cottonwood that grew between the two arms of the Ojo de los Brazos. "Why would God want to save this village?"

"*¿Quien sabe?*" Ramon would tell them, shrugging his shoulders. "One never knows. Perhaps in a thousand years, this place will amount to something." He would laugh and stroke his fingers through the black hair of one of the children. "That is God's business."

"Padre Ramon, tell us about Sister Petra."

His heart would throb and he would reply: "What do you want to know about her?"

"What did she look like?"

"Ay, muchachos," he would say, turning his palms to the brilliant New Mexican skies, his eyes sparkling like an ax against a grindstone. "She was the most beautiful woman you ever did see."

TOR

Award-winning authors
Compelling stories

Please join us at the website
below for more information
about this author and other great
Tor selections, and to sign up for
our monthly newsletter!